SHIRLEY ROGERS
COWBOYS, BABIES AND SHOTGUN VOWS

SILHOUETTE *Desire*

Published by Silhouette Books

America's Publisher of Contemporary Romance

To my husband, Roger, who believed in me.
And to Darlene, thank you for everything.

 SILHOUETTE BOOKS

ISBN 0-373-76176-7

COWBOYS, BABIES AND SHOTGUN VOWS

Copyright © 1998 by Shirley Rogerson

Memories Of Their Lovemaking Assailed Ashley, And She Sank Down On The Sofa And Wrapped Her Arms Around Herself.

What could one night hurt? Well, now she knew. Damn. If she hadn't gotten sick this morning, Ryder would never have known about the baby. He'd have gone back to his ranch and would have forgotten all about her.

But would she have forgotten all about him?

Ryder McCall had gotten to her somehow. How could she have slept with him again?

But she knew the answer to that. Chemistry. Whatever God had put in a woman and a man to attract them to each other, He'd given them a huge dose. There was something about Ryder McCall that Ashley just couldn't resist....

Dear Reader,

The perfect treat for cool autumn days are nights curled up with a warm, toasty Silhouette Desire novel!

So, be prepared to get swept away by superstar Rebecca Brandewyne's MAN OF THE MONTH, *The Lioness Tamer,* a story of a magnetic corporate giant who takes on a *real* challenge—taming a wild virginal beauty. THE RULEBREAKERS, talented author Leanne Banks's miniseries about three undeniably sexy hunks—a millionaire, a bad boy, a protector—continues with *The Lone Rider Takes a Bride,* when an irresistible rebel introduces passion to a straight-and-narrow lady...and she unexpectedly introduces him to everlasting love. *The Paternity Factor* by Caroline Cross tells the poignant story of a woman who proves her secret love for a brooding man by caring for the baby she *thinks* is his.

Also this month, Desire launches OUTLAW HEARTS, a brand-new miniseries by Cindy Gerard about strong-minded outlaw brothers who can't stop love from stealing their own hearts, in *The Outlaw's Wife.* Maureen Child's gripping miniseries, THE BACHELOR BATTALION, brings readers another sensual, emotional read with *The Non-Commissioned Baby.* And Silhouette has discovered another fantastic talent in debut author Shirley Rogers, one of our WOMEN TO WATCH, with her adorable *Cowboys, Babies and Shotgun Vows.*

Once again, Silhouette Desire offers unforgettable romance by some of the most beloved and gifted authors in the genre. Don't forget to come back next month for more happily-ever-afters!

Regards,

Joan Marlow Golan
Senior Editor, Silhouette Desire

Please address questions and book requests to:
Silhouette Reader Service
U.S.: 3010 Walden Ave., P.O. Box 1325, Buffalo, NY 14269
Canadian: P.O. Box 609, Fort Erie, Ont. L2A 5X3

SHIRLEY ROGERS

is happily married and lives in the Tidewater area of Virginia, where she was born and raised. Being one of five children, she says, gives her lots of experiences to draw on when writing her stories. She is the proud mother of a son and a daughter, both of whom are in college. In her free time she likes reading romances, traveling, seeing movies and shopping with her daughter.

The Silhouette Spotlight
"Where Passion Lives"

MEET WOMAN TO WATCH *Shirley Rogers*

What was your inspiration for COWBOYS, BABIES AND SHOTGUN VOWS?

SR: "I heard a song by Lorrie Morgan, and a line about understanding the word *no* just grabbed my attention. I could imagine the scene—a heroine being hit on by some jerk and having to think of a way out of a bad situation. The story just took off from there."

What about the Desire line appeals to you as a reader and as a writer?

SR: "I love the fast-paced, character-driven stories in the Desire line. They get to the heart of the reader and just won't let go."

What about this book is special to you?

SR: "As part of his character, my hero uses 'Darlin'' often. This came about because my brother, Lonnie, calls every woman 'Darlin',' whether he's opening a door for a stranger or talking to his wife, daughter or any other female. I've always thought that was sweet of him, and it just fit my hero, Ryder McCall."

One

Distraught because her father had tried to sell her into a love-less marriage, she hadn't been thinking straight.

"C'mon, li'l filly. A pretty thing like you shouldn't be sittin' all alone." Leering, the cowboy standing next to her lifted a long-necked bottle to his lips, chugged down the remainder of its contents, then swiped at his mouth with the back of his hand.

Ashley glanced around the dimly lit room and swallowed hard, thinking what an idiot she'd been to come inside this Podunk bar. She'd been exhausted when she'd stopped outside of Sonora and registered at the motel connected to the bar.

She'd paced in her room for a while, needing to calm her nerves before trying to get some sleep. The pills she'd taken from her stepmother's medicine cabinet should have made her relax. Over an hour later, she'd still felt wired. She'd come into the bar thinking a drink would help.

Since leaving San Antonio, she'd been in a continuous state of shock, stunned by the realization that her father had used her as a bargaining chip in a business deal and her fiancé had been a willing party to it. She'd spent her life trying hard to please her father and stepmother. And look where it had gotten her—in some hellhole with a drunken cowboy latched onto her.

Her head was beginning to ache and the country music from the band made her feel like a jackhammer was pounding away inside her brain. A woozy feeling rushed through her. She blinked hard, then took another, a much slower, look around, bringing the room into hazy focus. If she could just get her bearings, she'd get the heck out as fast as she could.

The smoke was thick enough to choke a horse, and the offensive odor stung her eyes and nostrils, creating havoc in her stomach. She started to get up, but stopped when the room slowly began to spin. Between the darkness and the smoke, she was barely able to make out the shadows of couples locked together on the small dance floor. Ashley flushed, swallowed the lump in her throat and glanced at the cowboy.

"I already told you no," she said, disgusted by the thought of him holding her like that. He didn't appear the least bit dissuaded. Tasting fear, she reached for the beer in front of her and took a drink for courage. She put the bottle down and was surprised it was nearly empty. She didn't remember finishing the first one.

"Oh, I un'erstand aw'right." The cowboy closed his hand around the back of her neck and leaned close to her, his foul breath making her gag. "You're a hot little number playin' hard t'get." His hand slid from her neck to her shoulder and squeezed it.

Ashley swung her arm at him in an attempt to push him away, but he snared her wrist in a tight grip. "Look, I'm waiting for someone," she snapped. It was the first thing that came to her mind. *Please, oh, please, leave me alone,* she prayed, trying to bank the panic taking hold of her.

Deke McCall stopped talking, aware that he'd lost Ryder's attention. He looked over at the bar, and his gaze took in the leggy female his older brother was watching. She was attractive in a ritzy sort of way, but far from the kind of woman his brother usually went for. Everyone who knew Ryder McCall knew he liked his women blond and voluptuous, not tall and whisper thin.

"Forget it, man."

Deke's words barely registering, Ryder's eyes narrowed as he watched the scene taking place at the bar. Apparently the cowboy was three sheets to the wind. It didn't look as if the lady was too happy with his attention.

"Oh, hell, Ryder," Deke growled. "Not tonight. I just came in here to unwind, not to get into a brawl."

Ryder's lips turned slightly upward, his teeth just showing beneath his trim mustache. "Looks like the lady needs some help."

Deke's expression turned pensive. "We're supposed to be in Bandera tomorrow to take a look at that Brahma bull. You mess this deal up and Jake's going to have your hide."

"Jake and who else?" Ryder quipped, undaunted by the warning about their older brother.

Seeing the uneasy look on Deke's face, Ryder tipped his hat up and looked him in the eye. "Quit worryin'. We'll leave bright and early in the morning. Right now I think I'll give the lady a hand."

Deke chuckled. "Yeah? Seems like I recall the last lady you rescued had a boyfriend the size of a Mack truck and you came away with two broken ribs and a black eye."

Ryder grinned, downed the last of his beer and set the bottle down on the small round table in front of him. He took another look at the woman at the bar. She sure was pretty. Silky black hair halfway down her back and a short black skirt that exposed long, lush legs. Something inside him sparked, an awareness so sudden and unexpected that he felt compelled to act on it.

Shifting his attention back to Deke, Ryder replied, "If your memory's so good, you'll remember he spent a couple of nights at County Hospital."

"And you spent the night in jail."

Ryder's blue eyes twinkled. "Only one night, little brother. The next night was well worth the fight." He winked and added, "See you in the morning."

Tugging his tan felt Stetson down on his forehead, Ryder strolled over to the bar with an exaggerated cowboy's gait. Without preamble, he laid a big hand on the drunken man's arm.

"Thanks for keeping my woman company," Ryder drawled, the cocky grin on his lips a direct contrast to the message his hard grip was giving the other man.

The cowboy's head snapped up and around. He let go of the woman and straightened, then swayed slightly. "Back off, buddy. I was here first."

Insinuating himself between the cowboy and the lady, Ryder draped his arm around the woman's tense shoulders. "The lady was just waiting for me. Ain't that right, darlin'?"

Ashley looked up and was swiftly caught in a baby blue gaze that made her feel dizzier than the couple of beers she'd consumed. The man was grinning, his white teeth smooth and straight beneath his dark blond mustache. Her thoughts were jumbled, but somehow she managed to sort them out.

Great, another cowboy. She put a hand to her head, the action seeming as if it was in slow motion. This night just wasn't getting any better, she thought. This guy was blond, at least six foot three and topped the drunk by more than four inches. His well-worn jeans rode low on his hips and gloved his body, sending out signals any red-blooded woman could pick up. He looked like a walking, talking advertisement for sex. When she started to speak, he leaned close and whispered in her ear.

"Play along with me, darlin', and you might just get out of here without causing a ruckus."

Ashley wasn't so sure. She didn't want to tangle with the drunk, but just looking into the seductive blue gaze of the man with his arm around her made her think twice about accepting his help. His iron-hard body generated a heat that seeped right into her, melting her resistance. Going totally on instinct, she managed a barely perceptible nod.

"See," Ryder pointed out, sending the woman a wink, "Like I said, she's been waitin' for me."

The cowboy snorted his disbelief. "You didn't just come in here," he said. "I seen you sittin' over there in the corner."

Ryder congenially smacked the cowboy on the back. "Well, buddy, there's a good reason for that. Let me buy you a beer and I'll tell you all about it." He raised his hand and caught the bartender's attention. The burly man promptly set three full bottles on the counter.

"You see, me and my woman had a little spat, and I came in here to blow off some steam. Ain't that right, darlin'?" he drawled, laying his Texas accent on thick. His gaze swept the woman's blank expression and he grimaced.

Ashley looked at the drunken cowboy, astonished he was falling for this crock of bull. She figured he'd consumed a lot more alcohol than she had. Still, it seemed smart to get rid of one problem and then handle another when and if it came along. She gave the new cowboy a small smile and slowly nodded.

"She just came in here to prove a point." Ryder turned and gave the woman a full-fledged smile, his eyes sparkling with amusement. "And you did that real good, darlin'. Made me jealous as hell."

He bent and lowered his mouth within inches of hers. "Give me a little kiss, darlin', and let's patch things up."

Ashley's eyes widened when they met his. Her gaze slid to his mouth. His upper lip was covered by that sexy mustache, and his lower lip was full and tempting. He inched a little closer and she smelled his enticing woodsy cologne and the faint scent of beer on his breath.

"C'mon, darlin'," he coaxed, then his lids lowered lazily, half covering his blue pupils. His hand on her shoulder gently prodded her toward him.

Ashley felt as if she was caught in a time warp. In a daze she lifted her mouth and touched her lips to his. His mustache tickled a little, but the feel of his mouth on hers made her heart tumble over.

A wave of warmth snaked through her, scrambling her senses, making her feel even more disoriented. Ashley found herself inching closer to him, being absorbed by the heat of his kiss, wanting more, needing more. She reached out to steady herself, settling her palm on his rock-hard chest.

Ryder groaned low in his throat as the woman laid her hand on him. He wondered for a split second just who intended to seduce whom. Arousal, hot and swift, soared through him. Her lips were soft and sweet and addictive—and screamed of innocence. Alarmed by his reckless response to her, Ryder removed her hand from his chest. He opened his eyes to find her staring at him, her expression so vulnerable she could have been an open book.

He looked at the woman who'd just kissed him and blinked. Her big brown eyes were guarded and apprehensive. He could tell she wasn't sure whether to trust him. He'd never deliberately hurt a woman, had never taken a woman who didn't know the score. He wasn't about to start now.

Turning back to the cowboy, Ryder grinned easily. "Can I buy you another beer?"

"No, thanks," the cowboy mumbled sullenly, grabbing a bottle of beer off the counter.

As soon as the man swaggered away, Ryder felt the woman beside him stiffen. He removed his arm from around her shoulders and slid onto the empty stool beside her. With his back to the bar, he braced his elbows on the ledge and turned to face her.

He stared at her for a moment. From a distance she'd looked like a society woman on the make. Checking his libido, he wondered for a moment if she was even old enough to drink. Though he still wanted her, at twenty-eight he was past the age where taking a virgin was considered a conquest.

Well, he'd started this and he'd see it through, even if the ending wasn't going to turn out the way he'd planned. Angling closer to her, he asked, "What's your name, darlin'?"

Ashley watched him suspiciously. He seemed harmless enough with that engaging smile, but her head was still spinning from his kiss, and she couldn't quite forget how much man came with it. "Ashley," she said cautiously, wondering if he noticed that she didn't offer her last name.

"Ryder McCall." He stuck out his hand. She looked down at it, then back up at his face. Ryder grinned like an alley cat on the prowl and said, "I don't bite."

Doubting that, Ashley took his hand. His palm and fingers were calloused, and she guessed he was a working cowhand from one of the nearby ranches. She drew her hand away and stared at the sweating bottle of beer in front of her.

"Thank you for what you did," she said, sending a nervous glance in his direction. His blue eyes sparkled. Embarrassed, she dropped her gaze to the counter.

"Glad to be of help." Ryder dipped his head until she was forced to face him. "Are you from around here?"

Ashley wasn't expecting the question. It took a moment for her to think of an answer that sounded reasonable. "No. I'm just passing through."

"Traveling alone?"

When she nodded, he frowned. Ashley tensed and hoped she hadn't aroused his suspicions.

"You shouldn't be traveling by yourself this late at night," he remarked, his expression curious. "How about I walk you to your car, just to be on the safe side?"

Ashley picked her purse up from the counter and clasped it in her lap. "Thank you, but that won't be necessary." She didn't mean to sound abrupt, but she didn't want him getting any ideas. As she slid off the stool, the motion carried her forward and off balance. "Oh," she murmured, her hand going to her forehead.

Ryder caught her against him and held her steady. "Hey, you all right?" He didn't think so. She looked a little green around the gills.

"I'm fine," she said, and wished she meant it. She clutched

his shirt and held on as if glued to it. Soon, very soon, she was going to get her equilibrium back, she told herself.

Ryder slipped his arm around her waist. "I don't think so." He held her tighter. Standing beside him, the top of her head came about to his shoulder. And she was so thin he could feel her ribs. He dug into his pocket and tossed some bills on the bar. "C'mon, darlin'," he urged and slowly moved toward the door. "I think some fresh air will make you feel better."

Afraid to let go for fear she'd pass out, Ashley leaned against him. When they reached the entrance to the bar, there was another cowboy standing in front of it, blocking their way.

"Oh no, not again," she murmured, nausea rushing through her stomach and damming in her throat.

Ryder grinned down at her. "It's okay. This is my brother, Deke."

Ashley had to force her head up. When she did, she met eyes identical to those of the cowboy who held her. Only these baby blues spoke openly of gentleness. He wasn't as tall, though, nor as muscular as the man holding her.

"Hello," she managed to say.

"Ma'am." He touched the brim of his hat.

"Get the door," Ryder said to his brother.

Not moving, Deke gave him a questioning look. "Maybe you've had more to drink than I thought."

Ryder straightened his spine, keeping his arm locked firmly around Ashley. "What the hell are you talking about?"

Deke nodded toward the girl. "She's jailbait."

"I'm just helping her outside." Ryder's look was indignant.

Deke raised an eyebrow. "That's all?"

"I swear," Ryder replied curtly. "I'll be back shortly." He met Deke's eyes with an expression of measured restraint. "Now, get the damn door."

Deke obliged, opening the door and stepping aside. Ryder guided Ashley through it and heard it close behind them. His gaze swept the dimly lit parking lot. "Which car is yours?"

Ashley drew a breath of night air, then willed herself to look up. "That one," she said, nodding toward her car.

Ryder started forward.

"Wait," Ashley murmured. "I don't feel so good." Her head was spinning and her stomach ached. "Please, just give me a minute."

Ryder grimaced when she trembled in his arms. "You shouldn't be traveling tonight."

Ashley felt as if the entire contents of her stomach were in her throat and she had a feeling she was going to embarrass herself very shortly. "I'm not. I have a room." Her hands shaking, she opened her purse and withdrew a key. She tried to read the number, but it swirled in front of her eyes. "Oh," she moaned again.

Ryder caught the key in his hand just as she dropped it. "C'mon." He urged her forward. They'd gotten as far as the backside of the motel when she stopped abruptly.

"I'm going to be sick," she confessed and groaned, pain ripping through her.

"We're almost there," Ryder said softly, encouraging her to continue. "Hold on."

Trying to steady herself, Ashley reached for the wooden post at the corner of the building. She bent over at the waist, her hand pressed against her stomach. "I can't. I'm s-sorry."

Ryder grabbed hold of her. "It's just another few steps," he whispered encouragingly. He put his arm around her and urged her to start walking. Then he heard another anguished moan and knew he was out of time. He tried to maneuver her to the nearest grassy area. "Hold on, darlin', hold on...hold on. Wait. Whoa, darlin', not my...boots," he groaned. Quickly, he grasped her long black hair and held it back from her face.

"Oh, my," Ashley wailed, realizing what she'd done. "Oh," she moaned again and grabbed her stomach as it cramped and twisted.

"It's all right," Ryder murmured, feeling sorry for her and a little sick himself. His arm was fast around her, supporting her slight weight. A few moments later he asked gently, "You finished for now?"

Ashley put a hand to her head. "I don't know." She took a step forward, then staggered.

Bending, Ryder swept her into his arms and carried her the rest of the way. She was soft and featherlight, easy in his arms. Checking the number on the key, he stopped in front of her motel room. He balanced her on his knee while he unlocked the door.

"I'm so sorry," she moaned, her eyes closed.

"Hush," he whispered, opening the door. Flipping on the light, he tossed his hat in a chair, then carried her through to the bathroom where he carefully put her on her feet.

Ashley opened her eyes and clutched the bathroom sink, her knuckles turning white from the strain of keeping herself upright. "I'll be all right now. Thank you."

Ryder wasn't paying attention. He ran the cold water and soaked a washcloth. Sitting on the toilet lid, he tugged her onto his lap, then gently bathed her face. He couldn't help worrying about her. She looked white as a sheet.

Ashley sank against him, appreciating his strength, his caring attention. She couldn't remember the last time someone took such care of her.

Ryder tossed the washcloth aside, then filled a nearby glass with water. "Here. Rinse and spit."

Automatically Ashley complied. She was too out of it to argue. Her mouth tasted better now and she faintly realized the water must have had something minty in it.

"How much did you have to drink?" Ryder asked.

Ashley's eyelids slid closed, then slowly opened again about halfway. She tried very hard to focus on her rescuer's handsome face. "Two."

"Two beers!" he repeated. "You're drunk on two beers?"

"Probably the medicine," she mumbled, then her eyes drifted shut again as a lazy, relaxed sensation stole through her.

Ryder's jaw tautened. "Medicine? What kind of medicine?" She didn't answer and he grasped her chin and lightly shook her head. "What kind of medicine, Ashley?" He let go and her head slumped against his shoulder.

Ashley's eyes remained closed. She was faintly aware of his voice calling to her. She wanted to tell him she'd be fine, to thank him and send him on his way. Exhausted, she just couldn't seem to find the strength to do it.

Ryder pressed his hand against her cheek and held her for a moment. Had she passed out or simply gone to sleep? Not sure, he carried her to the bed, tugged the covers down and lowered her to the mattress. He removed her shoes and dropped them on the floor beside the bed.

Now what? Ryder thought. Should I undress her? He ran a glance over her. The top button of her silky white blouse had come undone, exposing the soft swell of her breasts. Her skirt had slid up to the top of her thighs, scarcely protecting what it covered. Despite her innocence, he'd been in a state of arousal since he'd set eyes on her. Taking her clothes off would only aggravate the problem. Grimacing, he pulled at the top sheet and spread it over her.

She'd taken some sort of medicine. Ryder walked to the dresser, however there was nothing there but a wrinkled map. Spotting her suitcases in the corner, he rummaged through them. He held up something soft and silky—what there was of it—two thin straps and a scrap of creamy material. Groaning, he tossed it back in the suitcase. Finding nothing, he gave up.

Then he remembered her purse and retrieved it from the bathroom. Sitting on the edge of the bed, he spread its contents out. Immediately he spotted the brown bottle. Picking it up, he turned it over in his hand and read the label.

Valium.

Only, the prescription wasn't in her name. He tucked that away to think about later. Ryder's gaze swept over Ashley. Looking young and innocent, she lay sleeping. The sight of her touched something deep inside him. She needed someone, and he found himself wanting to shield her from the pain she'd sought to escape by taking pills.

"Darlin', what in the world landed you in the Blue Eagle Bar?" he asked aloud. And what on earth would a woman like her need to take Valium for? More importantly, how much had she taken? Swearing under his breath, Ryder stuffed her belongings back in her purse.

"Hell," he muttered, wondering what to do with her. He decided against calling a doctor, because he didn't really know if she'd taken too many pills. However, he didn't feel right leaving her alone. It seemed best just to keep an eye on her for a while.

Ryder unbuttoned his shirt and stripped it off, then walked around and sat on the opposite side of the bed. Sighing heavily, he reached for one of his boots, then stopped.

Hell.

Muttering a soft string of curses he removed both boots and strode to the bathroom to clean them. He washed up, turned off the lights and went back to the bed. He lay down, keeping to his own side, trying really hard not to think of what an alluring picture she made. Something inside his gut tightened, something he labeled lust. Propping his head against the pillow, he stared at the ceiling.

The next thing Ryder heard was the bed squeak. He opened his eyes, realizing he must have dozed off. He groaned and sat up, quickly looking around, adjusting his eyes to the darkness. A glance at the clock on the bedside table told him he'd been asleep for several hours.

"I didn't mean to wake you."

Ryder's gaze went to the direction of Ashley's soft voice. She was sitting on the edge of the bed, silhouetted by a beam of moonlight coming in from the cheap curtains on the window.

"How are you feeling?" he asked, concerned. His voice was hoarse. He attributed it to sleep rather than the fact that she'd changed into that tiny scrap of creamy silk. It glistened in the moonbeams and played havoc with his sanity.

"Better, but I'm still a little woozy." Ashley could still feel the effects of the beer or the medicine. Or, she wondered, did her light-headedness have something to do with the man beside her? Her stomach had calmed down and now it was her heart she was having trouble controlling.

"Why didn't you wake me?" Ryder asked.

Ashley looked at his face through the shadows. His concern touched a deep place inside her that she hadn't allowed anyone near in a long, long time. Besides her mother, who had died when she was young, no one had ever cared about her. Not really. "You were sleeping so peacefully." She lifted the covers.

"What are you doing?" Ryder asked. The pitch of his voice rose a little.

"Getting back into bed." Not looking at him, Ashley quickly slid under the covers, her heart pounding from his nearness and from what she was thinking.

Ryder sat up straighter, every muscle in his body tensing. "Are you used to getting into bed with strange men?" he asked tightly.

Ashley smiled in the darkness. She had never done anything like this before. She only knew that for once in her life she wanted to be more than Jacob Bennett's daughter. Tears came to her eyes as she remembered that she'd only been a bargaining tool for him. What a fool she'd been to believe her fiancé had cared for her. "Of course not," she whispered in the stillness that stretched out between them.

Ryder felt a strange sense of relief when he heard her answer. Still, he figured it was pure trouble for her to be lying so close to him with next to nothing on. "You're not afraid of me?"

Ashley settled on her side, facing him, her eyes searching what she could see of his expression through the moonlight illuminating the room. He seemed a little uneasy. Could it be that he felt the same magnetic pull between them that she did? She hung on to that thought.

"No."

Stretching out beside her, Ryder propped his head on his

hand. "Why not?" His voice was husky. He touched her dark hair, then picked up a strand and curled it around his finger. It was soft and silky and made him want to run his hands through it.

Ashley caught her breath. This man was a stranger and yet he wasn't. He'd been kind to her, had taken care of her. She didn't know why, but suddenly it didn't matter that they'd just met.

For once in her life she felt reckless, even a little bold. Maybe she was still under the effects of the medicine and beer. Maybe not. Maybe she was just reacting to Martin's betrayal. Or possibly she just wanted to be loved, just this once. She wanted a "night out of time" that she could tuck away in her heart.

"Because you took care of me," she answered simply. She touched her palm to Ryder's unshaven cheek. It was a little coarse, but beneath her hand she felt the tightening of his jaw. His warm breath fanned her wrist. "Do you do that often?"

Ryder's eyes connected with hers through the deep shadows. "What?"

"Rescue women." Ashley waited for his answer, her breath catching in her throat, her heart pounding so hard she was sure he could hear it.

"Sometimes," he said, and beneath his mustache his lips curved upward into a boyish grin.

"Do you usually end up sleeping with them?" she asked softly. Though he'd slept in her bed, they both knew that wasn't what she was talking about. The question ignited the air, and it crackled between them.

"I don't make it a habit."

"And now?" she asked in a whisper. Ashley moved closer to him, close enough to breathe in his male scent, close enough to see the pulse beating in his throat. She could feel his heat drawing her nearer still. Reaching out, she stroked his hard-muscled shoulder. She touched her hand to the small area of hair nestled in the center of his chest.

"Ashley." Her name came out on a groan. Ryder gently

grasped her wrist, intending to remove her hand from his body. Just the slightest touch from her and he was as hard as a rock.

"Darlin', no." Beneath his palm he felt the rapid beat of her pulse.

Hurt vibrated through Ashley and she drew away. "Why not?" she asked very quietly. Tears stung her eyes. No one had ever wanted her. Not for herself. Not for the person she was. Only because she was Ashley Bennett.

Ryder gently stroked her cheek with the back of his knuckles. "Don't," he said when he felt the dampness at the corner of her eye. She started to pull away and he stopped her, smoothing his hand down her back. "God, don't cry." He leaned over and brushed a featherlight kiss across her mouth, pulling away before he gave in to the temptation to taste her thoroughly.

She responded by sliding her arms around his neck. Ryder could feel the heat of her body against his own, the softness of her full breasts pressing against his chest through the silky material covering them. Suddenly she didn't seem so innocent. She looked like a woman. She felt like a woman. She tasted like a woman.

"You don't want this," he said, his voice husky with need, his body throbbing for her, his mouth only inches from hers.

"Yes," Ashley whispered, her heart in her throat, "I do. Kiss me. Please, Ryder."

Ryder liked the sound of his name on her lips. Too damn much. He wanted to hear her say his name in the throes of passion, wanted to hear her cry it out when he was deep inside her, so deep he would lose himself in her.

"Ah, darlin'," he groaned, "you don't know what you're saying."

Ashley strained toward him, lifting her lips to within a breath of his. "I want you. I know that," she answered.

Her hand stroked his face, then cupped the back of his neck and pulled his head down until her mouth touched his. Her tongue traced the line of his lip beneath his mustache, then flitted over his bottom lip, teasing his mouth open.

Ryder groaned and rolled on top of her, covering her mouth with his. Her heat consumed him as he slipped his tongue into her mouth and found hers. She met him timidly, yet her shyness and inexperience easily fueled the inferno that raged through his body.

Struggling for control, Ryder lifted his mouth. He licked his lips, still tasting her honeyed sweetness. His hands held her face so that she couldn't look away.

"There's more involved here than kissing, Ashley," he rasped, his breathing constricted. He hurt so bad he ached with it. He moved against her, his hardness pressing against her womanhood, only his jeans and a sliver of silk separating them. "I want you badly and that's where this is leading."

"I know."

Ryder took a deep breath and strained to stay in control, every muscle in his body taut. "I don't think you do. If we don't stop now, I can't promise I'll be able to."

"I don't want you to," she whispered, her breath warm and moist, her answer full of promise. She looked steadily into his eyes.

Ryder lowered his mouth to hers and kissed her upper lip, then slid his tongue slightly past her teeth, touching her tongue, teasing it, then sucking it into his own mouth. She arched against him as she kissed him back, her hands holding his face. Her mouth was unbelievably perfect, hot and satiny as his tongue stroked hers and urged her to give him deeper access.

He shifted his weight slightly off her and slid one tiny strap of her gown off her shoulder. His mouth left hers, then he slowly, methodically, bathed her neck and creamy shoulder with openmouthed kisses, his tongue tasting her salty skin. Everything about her assailed him at once—her enticing scent, her delicious taste, her total innocence. He felt her clutching at him, her hands and fingers flexing on his upper arms.

He slipped his hand beneath her nightie, tracing her rib cage until he encountered one soft, plump breast. The sound of her moan when he found her pebble-hard bud rippled through him.

He twirled it between his thumb and finger as he trailed hot, wet kisses down her neck. Ashley bucked beneath him, her hands sliding over his shoulders. Her fingertips squeezed his skin as she kissed the hot flesh of his neck.

Ryder slowly slid her gown up and exposed two round ivory globes. "I want to look at you," he said, then caught her wrists and raised her arms above her head. He touched his tongue to one tight rosy tip as he let her arms go and gathered one breast in his hand.

"Ryder," Ashley whispered, her voice breaking off when his rough tongue grazed her nipple. He laved it lavishly, then gently bit and tugged at it with his teeth.

Ashley had never felt anything so wonderful in her entire life. The sensations rippling through her were earth-shattering, yet so pleasurable, as if she were skydiving without a parachute. She wondered how anyone could endure such sweet torture and still live. Her body jerked when he moved to her other breast.

"Oh." She sucked in a hard breath when his teeth and tongue teased it, then was immediately aware that he'd lifted his head. She opened her eyes and found him watching her, his fingers gently rubbing where his mouth had been.

"Did I hurt you?" he asked, staring into her eyes.

"No." Her breathing was hard, but she managed to whisper, "Please, don't stop."

"I don't intend to."

Two

Ryder quickly rid himself of his jeans and underwear. His body met Ashley's again and he watched her eyes widen when he pressed his rigid length against her soft thigh.

"Are you sure?" he asked, his voice husky, giving her one more chance to pull back. He brushed her hair from her face so he could see her eyes.

Ashley slowly nodded without speaking. She couldn't find the words to tell him her body was still smoldering from the fire he'd started and left burning.

Ryder slid the gown the rest of the way off her and dropped it to the floor beside the bed.

"You're lovely," he rasped. His mouth covered one breast and he suckled her, then moved to give the other one the same wonderful attention, building the inferno inside her once more. She felt his hands, strong, yet amazingly gentle as he caressed and molded her.

Ashley's breath came harder as his mouth moved lower and lower. The gentle scraping of his mustache was tantalizing.

He drew his wet tongue over her skin, touching her with his mouth and teeth, teasing her body, making her want something wild and beyond her reach.

He kissed her belly, then focused his attention lower, his big hands running up and down her thighs. Her body moved in rhythmic motion as his finger moved between her legs and slipped inside her panties. For a fleeting moment, Ashley felt a sense of embarrassment when he found the moisture at the core of her. Her legs closed together and tightened automatically.

"Easy, darlin'," he coaxed, urging her legs apart with a gentle caress. "Just relax and let go. I'll take it slow." He leaned up and his mouth found hers as his palm covered her.

Ashley held his face with her hands and kissed him back as he removed her panties and began to explore her body. Liquid fire raced through her veins, and she called his name. Her legs fell open, awarding him even greater access as she writhed and twisted with every hot stroke of his fingers.

"Make love to me, Ryder," she pleaded. "Oh, please, please."

Ryder did as she bid and eased himself over her, holding himself above her with his arms, positioning his hard sex between her legs. It had been all he could do to hold himself back from taking her too soon, but he had wanted to be sure she was ready for him. He felt her body tense as he began to probe her. Though she hadn't said anything to warn him, he knew at that instant that she was as innocent as he had thought when he'd first kissed her.

"Relax, darlin'," he whispered, watching their bodies as he pressed into her. Bending down, he took her mouth in a deep kiss to distract her from the penetration of his body into hers. She was exceptionally tight, and he hesitated, then gently pushed again.

"Ryder," she whispered when he lifted his mouth.

"Darlin', you're so tight. I don't want to hurt you." Though he was ready to explode, he wasn't sure he could do this to her.

"I'm okay. Please," Ashley's sultry tone pleaded with him, and he felt her legs close tightly around his hips. She arched her body against his. The sudden movement caused him to push against her. She cried out, and then he was inside her. He remained still for a few moments, giving her time to accept the invasion of his body.

His tongue traced her mouth as he began to move, the fever between them igniting a fire that had barely cooled. He kissed her deeply, thrusting his tongue into her mouth, mimicking the movement of their bodies. Ashley's breathing became hard and fast. Her body tightened as he drove into her again and again, chasing the promise of ecstasy that was so suddenly within reach.

"Ryder. Ryder." Her nails scraped his back as she climaxed and called his name over and over again.

"Ashley, ah, yes, yes." Ryder gritted his teeth as his own body lost control. He closed his eyes and let himself slip over the edge and into the black void.

Bright morning sun peeked into the motel room through thin moss green curtains. Ryder stretched, rubbed the sleep from his eyes and rolled over and reached for Ashley. It took him a moment to realize he was in bed alone. He opened his eyes wider and sat up, slowly taking stock of his surroundings. The bathroom door was ajar, but there wasn't a sound coming from inside. A strange feeling crawled through his belly.

"Ashley?"

No answer.

Ryder told himself she'd probably gone out for coffee or something. He tossed the covers back and stood. It was then that he noticed her luggage was gone. For a moment his heart stopped beating.

"Ashley," he called again, this time his voice rising. He knew she wasn't in the bathroom, but he foolishly looked, anyway. He went back into the room and stared at the spot where her luggage had been.

She was gone.

His eyes searched the room for some sign that she hadn't been a figment of his imagination. Pulling on his clothes, Ryder cursed a blue streak that would have made his brothers blush. He checked the back pocket of his jeans, half expecting his wallet to be gone. Deke was never going to let him live this down.

Rolled by a virgin.

Hell.

He felt some consolation when he pulled out his wallet and opened it. His money, credit cards and identification were all there. Grimly Ryder jammed his wallet back into his pocket. He strode to the bathroom and splashed his face with cold water, thinking what a fool he'd been.

Back in the room he looked at the rumpled bed and the intimate sign that an innocent woman had shared it with him. This was worse than being rolled, he thought.

Seduced by a damn virgin!

Double hell.

Jerking his Stetson on, Ryder stepped outside the room. Though spring hadn't officially arrived, the unseasonably warm temperatures promised a Texas-hot summer day. With quick, long strides he walked to the room he was supposed to have shared with Deke. He let himself into the cool room, slamming the door behind him.

Deke shot straight up in bed from a dead sleep, his eyes flying open. "Ryder? What the hell?"

"I thought you wanted to get an early start," Ryder barked. He changed into a fresh shirt, then stuffed the rest of his things in his canvas bag.

Looking confused, Deke ran a hand through his short hair. "What time is it?"

"Time to get moving." His face set in a permanent frown, Ryder marched toward the door. "Meet me at the truck. You've got five minutes." He was out the door before his brother had time to respond. He covered the distance to the motel office in purposeful strides, his abrupt entrance instantly drawing the desk clerk's attention.

"I'd like some information about one of your guests," Ryder said, his voice gruff. "Room 112. The name and address of the woman who registered." Ryder strummed his fingers on the countertop, tapping out a thunderous beat.

"That information is confidential." The clerk shifted nervously under the bruising stare of the big man.

Ryder practically growled as he pulled out his wallet and slammed a twenty on the counter. He looked at the little man and glanced pointedly at the money. "The name and address." He figured the man could take the money or his fist. At this point he didn't really care which.

Eyes wide, the clerk quickly searched his files and handed the card over the counter.

Ryder stared at the small card. Ashley Smith. A fake name if he'd ever heard one. "No address?"

"She didn't list one when she registered." He shrugged his bony shoulders. "I figured it didn't much matter cause she paid in cash."

Ryder swore. Muttering obscenities under his breath, he stormed out of the motel office and headed for the parking lot to look for Ashley's car, knowing it wouldn't be parked next to his truck as it had been the night before. He remembered it was a late model Infiniti with Texas plates. He had a vague recollection of some of the numbers.

By the time Deke tossed his bag in the back of the truck and climbed into the cab, Ryder had the motor running. He jerked the gearshift into reverse and backed out, then slammed it into first. The truck took off as if it was being shot at.

"Who put a burr under your saddle?" Deke asked, glaring at his brother.

"Can it!" Ryder snapped. He didn't feel like talking. He felt like hitting something. He didn't want it to be Deke's jaw.

"I thought you were coming back last night."

"I thought so, too," Ryder admitted grimly.

Deke glanced at Ryder, then back at the highway. "I guess I don't have to ask where you were."

Ryder shot him a hard look. "I guess you don't."

"I thought you weren't going to take advantage of that girl."

There was a reproachful note in Deke's voice that, even through his fury, caught Ryder's attention. He had the feeling that his respect had slipped a few notches in his brother's eyes.

"It wasn't like that," Ryder said tightly, keeping his attention on the road. "Nothing was supposed to happen."

"Yeah, right. Tell me another one." Deke shifted and settled into the worn leather of his seat. "You've been loving 'em and leaving 'em ever since Ariel walked out on you."

Ryder shot Deke a wrathful stare, then turned back to driving. "This has nothing to do with Ariel," he denied, his voice harsh. Just the sound of his ex-fiancée's name dredged up bitter memories. It irritated the hell out of him that she still had the power to affect him two years after she'd humiliated him.

Deke didn't plan to let his brother off easy. "Quit lying to yourself. You might have wanted to play the hero last night, but you had ulterior motives from the get-go," Deke accused.

"Look," Ryder insisted, pushing thoughts of Ariel from his mind. "I'm the innocent party here. When I woke up this morning, she was gone. Lit out sometime during the night."

"What a hoot!" Deke chuckled.

"Dammit, it's not funny!"

"Oh, I don't know. I have a feeling Jake and the hands are going to find it hilarious when I tell 'em." Deke cackled, holding his gut.

Ryder glowered at him. "Go on and have fun. Just remember that if you open your big mouth, I'm gonna have to retaliate." His tone promised revenge in a big way. "I guess you don't mind anyone finding out about you and Mary Beth Adams."

Deke sat up, his back arrow straight as he removed his hat, his expression suddenly sober. "All right, all right," Deke said, sulking. "But it's not like you wanted to be saddled with her so what's the problem?"

Ryder growled, "There's no problem. No problem at all."

Except there was. Memories of the way Ashley had clung to him when he'd loved her that very last time raged in his mind. He couldn't forget the black-haired beauty, couldn't forget what had happened last night between them.

Dammit! He wondered if he ever would.

Three

Ryder stomped on the accelerator, swerved to the left of the paved two-lane road and passed a loaded-down flatbed truck. He couldn't get a grip on the restlessness inside him, and it was driving him crazy.

For four months he'd been as ill-tempered as a bull in a rodeo. Jake had finally given him an ultimatum—clean up his act or take some time off. Fuming, Ryder had chosen the time off. He'd headed down to Kinney County to negotiate the sale of some quarter horses, then spent a few days trying to find the mysterious raven-haired beauty he hadn't been able to forget.

Finding her had been like putting together a jigsaw puzzle. Pulling in a favor from a friend, he'd tracked the medicine bottle labeled in the name of Iris Bennett to San Antonio. He'd discovered that Iris Bennett was Ashley's stepmother, and that her father was Jacob Bennett, a well-known oil magnate. Further checking had shown that Ashley had been missing since the night he'd met her—the night that was supposed to have been her wedding night.

What the hell had she been doing sleeping with him when she was supposed to be married and on her honeymoon? Ryder cursed under his breath. Had she fooled him with her innocence and been out for a cheap thrill? Maybe for reasons of her own she'd set out to lose her virginity, and he'd been a means to an end. He had no idea, but she was going to answer some questions when he found her.

Ryder had put out a few feelers, and one of his friends had traced some activity on her savings account when she'd deposited money from her paychecks, money she'd earned working at a small diner. Though her account held a decent amount, it was far less than it should have been for someone whose father was worth millions.

His friend had also provided him with her address. That information had come to him just a few days before he'd found out she'd registered her car in the small town of Rocksprings in Edwards County. He'd cajoled another friend into periodically checking her records.

Now Ryder was just as uptight as when he'd left home. It all boiled down to that one night. One unforgettable night with a mysterious virgin.

Hell.

Why couldn't he forget? It wasn't just because she'd run out on him, though that had made him madder than a dog gettin' a bath. The morning after just wasn't supposed to end like that.

Ryder had had all the experience he'd cared to get when it came to becoming emotionally involved with a woman. After Ariel, he'd been determined never to go down that road again. Ariel had acted innocent, too—until she'd shown her true colors.

Ryder's jaw hardened. He could still hear her laughter when she'd told him she was too good to dirty her hands on a ranch. She'd taken pleasure in telling him she'd found someone else who had a lot more money and class than he had.

He'd been stunned, not believing he'd been so gullible. Stupidly, he'd persisted, asking her why she'd led him on, why she'd agreed to marry him. Her laughter still stung. She'd never intended to marry him. The sex had been good, she'd told him, but she could get that anywhere.

Ryder heard she'd gotten married only a couple of months after that to a man twice her age. He'd learned a bitter lesson from that experience and had tucked his heart safely out of reach. No woman was going to lead him down that road again.

Although, he had to admit he'd been awfully damn tempted that night with Ashley. He'd taken his time with her, shown her all the ways a man could please a woman. Exhausted, they'd finally fallen asleep and she'd snuggled up against him, fitting her body snugly inside the curve of his. As it turned out, she'd seduced him, used him, then she'd cut out behind his back.

Ryder figured it was male pride eating at him. It was a hard pill to swallow—knowing a woman had used him, when he thought he was too smart to let that happen again. It made him think about her even more, which made him madder than hell. He wanted some questions answered. Why hadn't she gotten married, and why had she been making love with him on what should have been her wedding day?

He turned off the country road when he finally saw a weathered sign advertising his destination, a diner just outside of Rocksprings, Texas. He was surprised to learn that Ashley had been living in this small town, only a few hours away from his family's ranch in Crockett County.

Ryder spotted Bess's Diner and turned into the dirt-and-gravel lot. Pulling to a stop, he got out of the truck and stretched.

He stepped into the diner and took a look around, his eyes searching for a tall, dark-haired woman. There was a long counter with faded red Formica. Metal stools lined the front of it, their red vinyl seats worn and discolored. Behind it was a huge grill and oven. A row of booths ran along the outside

wall, and a sign over the grill boasted The Best Home Cookin'
in the County.

His eyes narrowed when he spotted his quarry. He made his
way over to one of the booths, slid onto the seat and picked
up a menu propped between the salt and pepper shakers.

Ashley was waiting on an elderly couple when the customer
entered. She turned and started in his direction, then stopped
abruptly when she saw the way the cowboy's hat dipped low
on his head.

It can't be, she thought, her heart beating wildly. Her hands
started to shake and she nearly dropped the pad and pencil she
was holding. She stuffed them into her apron pocket, then
detoured and hurriedly walked behind the counter.

Stealing another look at him, Ashley let her eyes linger long
enough to verify she wasn't seeing things. It was him, all right.
Ryder McCall. What in the world was he doing here? Had he
been looking for her? She shook her head. Of course he
hadn't. Why would he? She'd only spent that one night with
him four months ago, and she was sure he wouldn't even
remember her.

"Better see to him," Bess suggested from behind her.

Ashley turned around and faced the owner of the diner, a
stout woman approaching middle age. Ever since Ashley had
come in asking for a job, Bess had treated her like a daughter.

"You wouldn't want to handle this one, would you, Bess?"
Ashley asked, her hand pressed against her stomach.

Bess gave her a steady look. "Well, that's going to be hard
to accomplish, seein' as how I've got to stay behind the grill."
She winked and added, "Besides, he's right handsome, don't
you think? With that blond hair to his collar and his hat and
mustache, he reminds me of one of them sexy country sing-
ers."

Ashley groaned, seeing no way out of the situation. She
rubbed her damp palms against her apron, took a deep breath
and walked over to his table.

"May I help you?"

Ryder looked up from the handwritten menu into the dark brown eyes that had haunted him for four long months. His gaze swept over the woman standing before him, taking in every dimension of her body. He remembered everything about her—her sweet taste, the way she moaned when his tongue stroked her breasts, the way she felt when she wrapped her legs around him.

Slowly his gaze came back to her face. A vision of them writhing naked together on the motel bed swam through his mind, and his mouth tensed just the slightest fraction.

His memory had served him well—he hadn't imagined, nor forgotten, how pretty she was. Her hair was still long, but instead of flowing free, it rested in a thick braid down her back. Her skin was still as smooth as silk, which made him remember how soft it had felt beneath his hands. His body tightened and he swallowed hard.

"The meat loaf special," he said, holding her gaze. "And coffee—black, no sugar." Ryder watched her turn and walk away. Her hips, encased in wash-worn denim, swayed slightly as she moved. Provocative. He remembered touching her hips, her thighs, remembered the way she'd begged him to sink into her that very last time. Ryder shifted, making room in his jeans by spreading his knees apart.

Hell.

He watched her as she worked behind the counter. She'd acted as if she didn't remember him. But she remembered. He knew she remembered.

Ashley filled a glass with ice and water after giving Bess the order for the special. Her hands trembled as she gathered the tableware. She took a deep breath and told herself to calm down.

Ryder had shown no sign of remembering her. She didn't know whether to be pleased or insulted. She hadn't really expected him to, but it hurt to think she'd been so forgettable to him.

It hadn't been that way for her. She'd thought about Ryder

a lot since that night. Their hours together had been incredible, at least they had been for her. Granted, it had been a crazy, dangerous thing to do. She wasn't the type to fall into bed with a stranger. But from the moment Ryder had walked up to her, Ashley had acted irresponsibly.

At first she'd blamed her actions on drinking beer while under the influence of medicine. She'd told herself that Martin's betrayal had driven her to sleep with Ryder. However, running away from her fiancé had only brought her to the bar. After a lot of soul searching, she'd finally admitted to herself she'd known exactly what she was doing that night.

A reminder of her carelessness was sitting right across the room. Muscular at the shoulders, lean at the waist, he was as handsome and virile as she remembered. She brushed a few strands of her hair from her forehead and walked back to his table. He looked up when she approached and snared her with his baby blue gaze.

"Your dinner will be right up." She put a glass of water and the tableware in front of him. Her eyes scanned his face, then swept over his body. He sat back and stretched one hard-muscled arm along the back of the booth. She looked at his big hands and thought about how gentle they'd been when he'd touched her, the thought making her feel weak and a little unsteady.

"Thank you, darlin'."

Ryder hadn't taken his eyes off her. Ashley went hot all over from his intense gaze. Her tongue slipped out and wet her lips. "Can I get you anything else?"

Ryder's mouth curled slightly in one corner, a teasing amount of his teeth showing beneath his mustache. "Well, darlin', it's right sweet of you to offer. I might take you up on something more later."

Ashley felt a blush rising from deep within her. She hurried back behind the counter to the sinkful of dishes. Bess, busy cooking an order, looked up when Ashley approached.

"He giving you a hard time? If so, I'll call Slade."

Ashley frowned and shook her head. "I'm all right." Slade

Carter was the local sheriff. She'd met him when she first came to town, and he'd been kind to her, telling her about the job at Bess's and introducing her to Miss Tilley, from whom she'd rented a room. He'd asked her out a couple of times, but Ashley had refused. Right now only Bess knew about the baby she was carrying. "There's no need to call Slade."

Concerned, Bess frowned. "You sure? He'd come in a hurry, you know. He stops in every morning just to get a look at you."

"Bess, stop talking like that. You know there's no future in it. Slade and everyone else in town will soon know that I'm pregnant." She'd already confided some of her problems to Bess. It had felt good to talk with someone who wouldn't judge her, someone who would just listen and offer advice if asked. Ashley stuck her hands in sudsy water and started washing glasses.

"He's a good man and it may not matter to him. You could do worse."

Ashley rolled her eyes. "Bess."

"All right, all right. I won't say nothin' more." She started putting food on a clean plate. "Tell me about *him,*" Bess said.

Ashley looked over at Ryder and her heart stopped. She hadn't thought she'd ever see the baby's father again. What was she going to do? Before she could give it further thought, Ashley heard the bell ring above the door and dried her hands. "Not now. I've got customers to wait on." She headed for the booth where a young couple had seated themselves.

For the next few minutes Ashley stayed busy waiting on customers. She'd glanced Ryder's way a couple of times and caught him watching her. He hadn't acknowledged he knew her. She couldn't believe how much it bothered her.

After serving his dinner, she'd given him his check, thinking he'd leave. Instead he'd stayed and ordered dessert. Near the end of the dinner rush, she went over to clear his table and he caught her wrist before she could move away.

"Sit down for a minute, Ashley."

Ashley's gaze flew to his eyes and she saw recognition in

them. And something else, something deep and smoldering. Her stomach did a somersault.

"I'm busy."

"Sit," Ryder commanded and tightened his grip.

Ashley glanced around the room. The only two customers left were sitting at the counter where Bess could wait on them. Hesitantly Ashley set the dishes back on the table and slid onto the seat opposite him.

"We need to have a little chat," Ryder said, releasing his hold on her.

Ashley slowly moved her head from side to side. "I don't think we have anything to talk about."

Ryder propped his booted foot on the seat next to her, effectively pinning her in. He gave her a questioning look. "Let's start with your name. Or do you really expect me to believe it's Smith?" He wanted to know if she'd tell him the truth.

Ashley dropped her gaze. "We're strangers. What difference does it make?"

"We're hardly strangers." Ryder leaned forward and touched her chin. He lifted her face until she met his eyes and couldn't look away. "We were strangers when I walked up to you in that bar. Now? Darlin', I know every inch of you. I know what it's like to kiss your mouth. I know what it feels like to be inside you."

Ashley flushed and jerked her head back. "Don't talk to me like that."

Ryder put his hand over hers and stroked her smooth skin. "Why not? You liked it when—"

"Stop it!" she cried. She snatched her hand away and glanced around nervously.

Ryder sat forward and laid his cards on the table. "I want to know why you took off without a backward glance. I thought we'd shared something special that night." At the time he'd looked forward to spending a few more nights with her.

Surprised by his words, Ashley replied straight-faced, "We

had sex. Don't try to make me believe it meant something more to you.''

"Are you telling me it meant nothing to you?" Ryder countered, his voice hard as granite.

Ashley scrambled to her feet. "Think about it. We didn't even know each other. What else could it have been?" she asked, trying to keep her voice down.

Ryder got to his feet and towered over her. Anger swelled inside him, blocking out all reasonable thought. "Look," he said hotly, "I'm not some easy lay!"

The whole diner fell quiet. Ryder looked around the room and realized they had quite an audience. He felt himself turning red and cursed under his breath, not believing he'd said something so stupid.

She was making him crazy.

"Shh!" Ashley cried, glancing frantically at the two men and Bess, who were openly staring in their direction.

Ryder grabbed his hat and stuffed it on his head. "What time do you get off?"

"I don't want to see you."

"Well, that's just tough, lady. I figure you owe me some answers and I aim to get them. Now, what time do you get off?" he demanded again.

"Seven!" Ashley hissed, her eyes torches of fire as she glared at him.

Pulling out his wallet, Ryder tossed some bills on the table. "I'll be here at seven." He turned and stomped out of the diner.

The silence in the room seemed to swallow Ashley up. She concentrated on collecting the dishes and tried to put Ryder McCall out of her mind.

He refused to go, thoughts of him staying with her for the remainder of her work day.

Ashley carried the dishes to the sink and began cleaning up the diner, ignoring the stares from the men at the counter. What was she going to do about Ryder? He didn't act as if he was going to settle for some glib reasons for what happened between them. Ashley had left that morning because she was too embarrassed to tell him the truth, that she'd foolishly turned to a stranger when she'd caught her fiancé in bed with another woman.

What she had shared with Ryder had been honest and pure, and, as silly as it sounded, she'd fallen just a tiny bit in love with him. She'd realized how very naive she was about that. It was natural for a woman to have feelings for the man who initiated her in sex, especially if the man was as handsome and charming as he was. However, now, of course, she realized that it had been more hormones than anything else. She couldn't love someone she didn't even know.

The first moment she'd laid eyes on him Ashley had feared he would be trouble to her heart. He'd rescued her, then, after realizing she was sick, he'd taken her back to her room to care and watch over her.

Ashley couldn't remember ever having felt so special. Her mother had died when she was very young and her father had remarried shortly after. The ensuing years were difficult for her. She could never seem to please her stepmother. She was never pretty enough, graceful enough, smart enough.

By the time Ashley was in her late teens, her stepmother had become totally domineering. When Ashley had asked for permission to date a boy from school, Iris Bennett had been furious. She claimed he was far beneath her standing. Crushed and desperate, Ashley had appealed to her father for help.

Jacob Bennett didn't have time to deal with her foolishness. She'd had advantages that most girls only dreamed of. He as much as told her to stop feeling sorry for herself and to obey her stepmother. She was a Bennett, he'd sternly reminded her. She was to act like one.

In defiance, Ashley had refused to date any of the young men her stepmother suggested. Iris had a low tolerance for disobedience. Ashley had been locked in her room for two days without meals. Shown just how cruel Iris could be, Ashley eventually decided it was healthier and safer to give in to her demands.

Later, Ashley met Martin Edward Collins, Jr., at a party given for her father's birthday. Martin was well-bred and very sought after. Ashley opened up her heart once again, and Martin seemed to really care for her. When he rushed through courting her and asked her to marry him, Ashley had accepted his proposal. Though not wildly in love, she truly cared for him. Admittedly, she also saw the marriage as a means of getting out from under Iris's iron rule.

On the night before her wedding, Ashley had overheard Martin and her father talking. Bennett Enterprises was actively seeking a merger with Collins, Incorporated. As one, the two oil companies would have a monopoly on supplying half of the resources used by their region of the United States. A marriage between Ashley and Martin would keep it in the family. Ashley realized she'd been sold to Martin, just like a piece of property.

Though deeply hurt by her fiancé's motives and her father's greed, she'd convinced herself to go through with the marriage. There were fates much worse than being married to a handsome, successful businessman: namely, continuing to live under her stepmother's tyranny.

The next morning she'd gone to Martin's room to tell him she'd overheard the conversation. She'd walked in and found him in bed with one of the maids. Something inside Ashley died at that moment.

She'd hurled Martin's engagement ring at him and gone back to her room to grab the cases she'd packed for her honeymoon. She'd taken off and hadn't stopped until she'd pulled into the parking lot of the cheap roadside motel several hours later.

"Ready to lock up?" Bess asked, interrupting Ashley's thoughts.

"Oh. Yes, of course." Ashley took off her apron and hung it on a nail by the back door. She rubbed her palms against her denim-clad thighs.

"You gonna be all right?" Bess was watching her closely.

"He's out there, you know. Been sitting in his truck for the past fifteen minutes. You seein' him?"

"I need to find out what he wants," Ashley answered. "You've been really kind to me, Bess. I appreciate everything you've done, letting me have this job until your daughter gets out of school." She smiled sadly. "I don't want to leave you without help, but it may become necessary."

"Jolene only has a couple of weeks of school left. Have you thought of what you're going to do for a job then?"

"I've been asking around. Slade said the sheriff's office in Kinney may have an opening for a receptionist. He's going to check on it for me," Ashley said.

"You can't keep running," Bess chided gently. "Sooner or later the past catches up with you."

Ashley looked out the diner window and whispered, "I'm afraid it just did."

Four

Ryder slid out of his truck and slammed the door behind him. A fine layer of dust covered his boots as he stepped up onto the sidewalk and watched Ashley come out of the diner. She met his eyes briefly, then her gaze skirted to the woman with her.

"This is Bess Cooper. Bess, Ryder McCall."

Ryder touched the brim of his hat. "Ma'am."

Bess gave him a polite smile before she turned to Ashley. "You gonna be all right?" she asked, deep concern in her voice.

Ashley touched Bess's shoulder to ease any misgivings she had about leaving her with Ryder. "Yes, of course." She had no idea what Ryder wanted of her or what possessed him to stick around, but she was certain she wasn't in any physical danger.

"I'll see she gets home safely," Ryder assured Bess, and gave her one of his most endearing grins.

"You'd better," she warned gruffly, giving him a meaningful look. "The sheriff is a good friend of ours."

There was a wealth of warning in Bess's tone and Ashley smiled at her friend's protectiveness. It made her long to have grown up with a mother as sweet and as kind as Bess.

"Good night, Bess. I'll see you in the morning."

The woman was slow to turn and walk away from them. Ryder motioned toward his truck. "Hop in. I'll give you a lift."

Ashley looked at the truck, then back at Ryder, and nausea attacked her stomach. She didn't think she could handle being with him in the confines of the cab. Her emotions had been in turmoil since he'd walked into the diner, and her pregnancy was beginning to take its toll on her. She shook her head and gestured down the nearly deserted street. "It's a nice evening and only a short walk."

"Lead the way." Nodding his head, Ryder took her arm. He frowned when Ashley made it a point to pull away from him. She started toward the north of town and he matched his usual long stride to her smaller steps. He'd heard the admonition in Bess's tone when she mentioned the sheriff and wondered why she'd felt the need to protect Ashley from him. Had Ashley given Bess some reason to fear he might be a threat to her?

He didn't want to believe she had. Then again, she'd said and done everything she could to try and make him leave. Maybe Ashley was afraid of him.

Ryder mulled that over for a few minutes, then the thought struck him that maybe Bess was trying to tell him something else. Was there something between the sheriff and Ashley, something personal, even intimate? It nagged at Ryder as they walked in silence.

"What did you tell her about me?" he finally asked, unable to contain himself.

"Who? Bess?" she asked, then added, "Nothing." Ashley tucked her hands into the front pockets of her jeans, still making it a point not to look at him.

He cocked an eyebrow, finding her answer impossible to believe. "Then why did I get that warning about the sheriff?"

They crossed the narrow street and stepped onto the sidewalk. "Bess is like a mother hen," Ashley told him. "I'm sure she didn't mean anything personal. I've made some good friends here. People in small towns tend to look out for each other." Ashley looked toward the sun. Low on the horizon, it filled the western sky with an amazing orange glow.

Ryder stopped walking, took hold of her arm and brought her around to face him. "Exactly how *good* a friend is the sheriff?"

Ashley stared up at him. "Why do you want to know?"

Ryder's mouth tightened, slightly twisting his mustache. "Just answer the question."

"He helped me find a job and a place to live when I first came to town," she explained, turning her head away from him. She brushed a wisp of hair behind her ear.

Ryder followed the motion with his eyes. He remembered how soft her touch had been on his skin the night they'd made love, and his body tightened with that same consuming need. "That's all?"

He couldn't shake the feeling that she wasn't being straight with him. She'd looked away when she'd answered him, making him wonder if she was telling him the truth.

Ashley's back stiffened. She didn't like his tone. It implied a lot more than just the simple question. "Exactly what is it you want to know?" She took in his set features, his questioning eyes, the wrinkles of a frown on his forehead. Her eyes went cold. "You're asking if I'm sleeping with him!" she stated, her tone sharp with accusation.

Ryder didn't even try to deny it. "Are you?" he demanded.

Indignation registered on her face, then a surge of fury began to build deep inside her. It didn't take long for it to swell to the point of exploding. "That's none of your business!"

From the determination on his face, Ryder wasn't about to let the subject drop. "Are you?" he asked again, undaunted.

The rosy flush in Ashley's cheeks came from the rage racing

through her. She stared him down, her stance rigid, her expression defensive. "Oh, let me see if I've got this right. I slept with you the first time we met so you're assuming I'll jump in bed with anyone." Her eyes darkened with anger and frustration, and despite her efforts to hide it, the hurt was there, also.

"You're putting words in my mouth," Ryder countered, a slight edge to his voice. He was finding out that losing his temper around Ashley was easy. She had a way of pushing his buttons. "I didn't accuse you of anything," he grated out, then his voice gentled. "I haven't forgotten you were a virgin the night we spent together. I think that's proof enough that you don't sleep around. I just want to know if you're involved with the sheriff."

Ashley couldn't believe his nerve. She stared him straight in the eyes, brown fury meeting his intense blue gaze. "You have no right to ask me personal questions. I can sleep with any man I choose. As a matter of fact, I can sleep with a hundred men if I want to, and you don't have the right to say one word about it. Get that straight right now, mister! I won't live under anyone's thumb ever again, and I don't have to answer to you or anyone else."

Ashley could have kicked herself for revealing what she did. She'd always held her temper under control, because Iris had some pretty despicable ways of disciplining her. Ryder had the power to undermine her and shake her up, and she didn't like it one bit.

Ryder reached for her, and she swatted his hands away. "Just keep away from me, Ryder," she fairly shouted, punching her finger into his hard chest. "If you're just passing through, then do it and get out of my life. I don't need you. I don't need anybody."

Her tirade over, Ashley swung around and marched away from him, up the street and toward Miss Tilley's. Tears burned her eyes and she brushed at them with her palms. God, she didn't need this! She didn't need more complications in her life.

She'd learned the hard way not to trust men and Ryder McCall added up to more proof. She didn't want to give him an inch, because he seemed the type to take a mile. She wasn't going to give up her child, and she was afraid that if he knew about it, he'd fight her for it. How could she have been so careless?

Hurrying toward home, Ashley didn't have to think hard to remember every single detail of that night. It was a time out of sync with the rest of her life. She'd finally decided she could make her own decisions, decide her future, put the past behind her.

Well, she'd botched that pretty good. She'd done something she'd wanted for once and she'd ended up pregnant. Her one big decision would affect the rest of her life.

The responsibilities of raising a child alone weighed heavily on her. Could she really do this? she wondered for the thousandth time. Bringing a child up with two parents was hard enough these days. There was no way she'd access her bank accounts in San Antonio. Besides not wanting to use her father's money, she was afraid he'd use the activity on her accounts to trace her to Rocksprings. She'd been able to save some money while working with Bess, and she'd started looking for a permanent job. Once she was settled, she could take some courses to better her situation. She was determined to take care of herself and her child.

Her baby would never know scorn and ridicule. She'd shower it with love and affection. And her baby would love her back. Together, they'd be a family.

Except now Ryder had shown up to cause even more problems.

Ashley had reached the boardinghouse and had started up the steps to the porch when Ryder grabbed her arm and spun her around to face him. As she tried to break away, he pinned both of her hands with his, holding them behind her back, the action bringing her body flush against him. Ashley tried to wriggle free without succeeding.

"Whoa now, darlin'. Don't get so riled." His voice low

and husky, Ryder coaxed her to his will as if she were a wild
pony. In ways he was yet to understand, she seemed hell-bent
on chasing him from her life. Well, he had a thing or two to
say about that, wondering about her motives. He'd be damned
if he'd leave until he was good and ready.

He wrestled with her another minute or so before the fire
seemed to go out of her. When she looked up at him, Ryder
saw desperation and panic in her eyes. And tears. His stomach
tightened. He didn't want to be the one to put tears in her
eyes.

Once she was in his arms, Ryder realized just how much
she'd changed since he'd last held her. He remembered how
thin she'd been the night they'd made love, as if she hadn't
taken very good care of herself. Since then she'd filled out
nicely. Her body was soft and feminine, her scent the same as
that long-ago night. She was breathing hard, and her breasts
pushed intimately against his chest.

Ashley stopped struggling, and Ryder relaxed his arms
without letting her go. Her body seemed to melt right into his.

"Look, I'm sorry," he said, his tone soft and cajoling.
"Maybe it isn't any of my business." Ryder cradled her
against him, his legs spread, her stomach nestled snugly
against him.

"Maybe?" Ashley squared off with him, her expression de-
fiant as emotions she wasn't ready to face whirled through
her. Her legs felt weak and her heart shuddered at his nearness.
She looked into his blue eyes, and his fierce gaze made her
hot and achy all over.

It hadn't been the reaction she was expecting and it took
her by surprise. She wanted to stay angry at him, wanted him
to leave her alone, wanted him to take off before he found out
she was carrying his baby.

Something changed between them at that moment and Ashley went completely still. Gazing into his eyes, she was reminded of soft touches and warm, sweet kisses, of passion so
hot and fierce it burned out of control. She'd told herself to

forget about what it had been like with him, but like a bad ache, it was there inside her, pulling at her.

Ashley wasn't a naive girl anymore. Ryder had shown her how many ways a man and a woman could please each other. He'd been worldly and full of experience. His eyes softened and his pupils dilated. She knew desire was mirrored in her own eyes. Embarrassment flooded her.

Before she glanced away, Ryder saw the longing she fought so hard to conceal hidden in the depths of her dark eyes. Whatever demons she was fighting, she couldn't deny there was a spark of something between them.

Knowing better than to react to the sensual tension building between them, he tried to defuse the situation instead. He grinned slightly, which turned his mustache up at one corner of his mouth. "Maybe," he conceded.

His gaze slid to her lips and he ached to lower his mouth to hers. He remembered the way she tasted. Hot. And sweet, so sweet and moist. He wanted to see her passion flare for him again, her desire rage out of control for him.

Ashley looked back at him. "Let me go. Please," she pleaded, desperation lining her voice.

Letting her go was the last thing on Ryder's mind. Her body was pressed against his, and he could smell the soft fragrance of honeysuckle in her hair. He remembered only too well that it had felt like silk as it slid across his chest when he was deep inside her. He wanted that again. Badly.

"Promise you won't take off."

Ashley drew a deep breath, her body suddenly on fire for Ryder. It scared her, this strong emotional pull he had on her. He had the ability to make her feel things she didn't want to feel, ache for something beyond her grasp. She was trying to straighten out her life, not make it more complicated.

"All right, I promise. Now let go." Ashley had no intention of keeping her word. As soon as he released her she was going inside the house and locking the door.

She pushed out of his arms, but before she could make a move, the screen door behind her opened and a tall, thin woman stepped out on the porch. She wore a cotton print dress, and her silver hair was twirled up in a maidenly bun at the back of her neck.

"Ashley, dear. I was just wondering where you were." The woman caught sight of Ryder at that moment and rushed on, "Oh, I didn't realize you had a gentleman caller."

Ashley turned her back on Ryder. "I'm sorry, Miss Tilley. I should have called to let you know I'd be a little late."

"That's quite all right, dear."

Ryder took his hat off and nodded at the older woman. "Good evening, ma'am," he greeted her.

Miss Tilley was openly curious and Ashley felt it necessary to set straight any foolish notions Miss Tilley had about Ryder. He most certainly was *not* a gentleman caller. "Miss Tilley, this is Ryder McCall. He's uh…an…acquaintance of mine."

"It's a pleasure to meet you, Mr. McCall." Miss Tilley came forward and shook Ryder's hand.

"The pleasure's mine," he said and gave Ashley a confused look. "Please call me Ryder," he insisted.

Miss Tilley smiled, then turned toward Ashley. "I've already finished eating, but I kept a plate warming for you. Perhaps your friend would like to join you," she suggested.

"He's already—"

"That's right nice of you to offer, ma'am," Ryder said, interrupting Ashley. "Are you sure I wouldn't be intruding?"

"Of course not," Miss Tilley replied, her tone cordial. "There's plenty left over from supper."

Holding his hat in his hand, Ryder motioned for Ashley to precede him, then followed behind her. The rambling old house had worn wooden floors, and the foyer had a staircase that led upstairs.

"Ashley, perhaps you'd like to freshen up. I'll show Ryder to the washroom in back."

Ryder stepped around Ashley. "Thank you, ma'am."

Ashley stared after them as they walked toward the kitchen, listening as their voices faded away. She stomped up the squeaky stairs to the bathroom and practically slammed the door behind her.

What was she going to do now? She didn't want to go downstairs and eat dinner with Ryder McCall, but had little choice in the matter. Miss Tilley had gone to the trouble to keep her dinner warm; she did so often, insisting that since Ashley worked in a diner, she shouldn't have to eat there, also.

Gathering her composure, Ashley studied herself in the mirror as she washed up. She didn't look pregnant. Who would have thought that one night's indiscretion would have caused her this much trouble?

Well, no matter what happened, Ashley was happy about the baby. And no one was going to come between her and her child. Not even this handsome, sweet-talking cowboy.

With that thought, Ashley headed back downstairs, determined to get rid of him. Moments later, she walked into the kitchen. Ryder was seated at the table, his long legs stretched out, his boots crossed at the ankles. He straightened when he saw her. Ashley was forced to sit next to him when Miss Tilley put her plate beside his on the table.

"Come on and sit down," she called. "Do you live around here, Ryder?" she asked as she filled two glasses with ice and tea.

"My family owns a spread over in Crockett County. It's a couple of hours or so from here," he explained.

"Family?" Ashley blurted out, nearly choking on a bite of food. He couldn't be married. Her gaze went to his hands, searching for a ring. They were large and strong, a working man's hands, but he wore no jewelry, nothing to indicate that he belonged to another woman. She hadn't asked him that night, had assumed he wasn't. Now her heart hung in limbo while she waited for his answer.

Ryder looked at her as if he'd read her mind and was contemplating her thoughts. "I have two brothers and a sister."

"You're not married?" she asked bluntly, holding her breath.

Ryder scoffed. "Nope."

Ashley breathed a deep sigh of relief. At least she had that to be thankful for. She didn't think she'd ever be able to trust her own judgment if she'd slept with another woman's husband.

"You live with your family on a ranch?"

"Yeah. You met my youngest brother, Deke, that night at the bar."

"I did?"

"Yeah, only you weren't feeling too good by then, so I'm not surprised you don't remember."

Miss Tilley put the filled glasses in front of them. "She hasn't been feeling too good the past few mornings, either," she volunteered. "I hope you're not coming down with something, dear."

"I'm not," Ashley insisted. Her gaze flew to Ryder's face, but his expression didn't change. Somehow that didn't make her relax. Right now she had control of deciding what was best for her and the baby. She had a small savings account, money she'd put away a little at a time. If she was frugal, it was enough to hold her until she found a permanent job. The last thing she wanted was Ryder's interference.

What if he put two and two together? Her heart pumped harder. She took a deep breath and tried to calm down. She was just being paranoid. He didn't know about the baby.

"Well, I hope not," Miss Tilley continued. "You haven't forgotten that I'm leaving in the morning to visit my sister?"

"I'm fine, really," Ashley insisted. "You go and have a good visit."

"If you're sure." Miss Tilley left the room, telling them she was going to bring in laundry from the clothesline.

Alone with Ryder, Ashley shifted uncomfortably as she thought about how to broach the subject of the night they'd spent together. If nothing else, she certainly owed him an apology for her abrupt departure. "Um, about that night. I'm really sorry about what happened." She lifted her glass and focused on its contents.

Ryder nodded, but it was clear he had questions he wanted answered. "Why'd you do it?"

Ashley's gaze flew to his eyes and she tried to read his thoughts. "Do what?" she asked, finding it hard to swallow. She picked at her food for a moment, then put her fork down.

"Why'd you mix the pills with booze? Did you have a death wish or something?"

Ashley's mouth dropped open. "No, of course not! I just wasn't thinking. I'd had a pretty big shock earlier and I'd taken something to calm me. When it didn't work, I didn't think there was any harm in having a beer."

"Well, it was a damn fool thing to do." Ryder hadn't forgotten how worried he'd been when he'd found the pills.

"I didn't know it was going to affect me like that."

Ryder pushed his plate away and touched her hand with his. He wanted her to confide in him, to tell him why she'd spent the night with a stranger, why she hadn't gotten married. "You were pretty sick," he commented. "Are you all right now?"

Ashley snatched her hand back. "Of course I am. I was fine the next day."

Ryder frowned. "Well, I wouldn't know about that. You didn't stick around long enough for me to find out, did you?" His tone held an accusation.

Guilty as charged, Ashley diverted her gaze. "Look, I think it's best if we just forget that night ever happened."

Ryder's expression nearly turned to stone. She sure seemed bent on getting rid of him, forgetting he ever made love to her. Why? he wondered again. What was she hiding? He began to speak, but stopped when Miss Tilley came back into the room and deposited her laundry on the counter.

"Oh, I see you're finished. Can I get you something else?" she asked them both.

"No, ma'am." Ryder complimented her on the meal, and the old woman glowed.

She looked at Ashley. "Why don't you take Ryder out on

the porch and sit for a spell. There's a real nice breeze to-night.''

When he saw Ashley getting ready to make an excuse, Ryder replied, ''That's a great idea.'' He got to his feet and held the back of her chair.

Ashley shot him a hot look and led the way outside. Ryder grabbed his hat and followed her. The screen door squeaked when he eased it shut. Spying the porch swing, he walked over and sat down. After balancing his hat on the railing, he patted the space beside him. ''Come on and sit beside me. I promise I won't bite.''

Ashley watched him warily. If he'd expected it to be easy to flush a few details out of her he was learning differently. Her manner cautious, she walked over and sat on the swing, keeping as much distance between them as possible.

Ryder started the swing rocking with the heel of his boot, and evening settled around them, bringing with it the sounds of the night insects, the whisper of a warm summer breeze.

Puzzled by the woman beside him, his mind naturally wandered back to the night they'd met. They'd shared an evening of intimacy together and he knew every inch of her body but little else about her. She'd run away from him as if her very life had depended on it. She hadn't given him a chance to get to know her, hadn't waited to see if he wanted to. Hell, she hadn't even told him her last name. And she was being awfully evasive now.

Ryder reached over and took her hand in his. She resisted at first, but he held on to her, refusing to let go. He could feel her pulse race beneath his fingers, and he stroked her hand. Finally he couldn't stand the silence any longer.

''Who are you running from, Ashley?''

Five

Ashley's eyes connected with his and she wanted to look away. Her first instinct was to flee inside the house and hide. But she'd made changes in her life and she wasn't going to let Ryder McCall bully her. She lifted her chin, staring him in the eyes.

"I'm not—"

"Don't even try it," Ryder told her, cutting her off. "I know your name is Ashley Bennett and you're from San Antonio. I also know that not too long ago you were engaged to be married. What I don't know is why you were at the motel that night." He reached over and stroked a finger down her cheek. "So what happened?"

Moving her head, she drew away from him. Just the slightest touch from him made her feel warm and womanly, and she couldn't afford to give in to those feelings.

"How did you find out my name?" she asked, and felt the panic rising inside her despite the fact that she'd been gone from her home four months and no one had come looking for her. If Ryder, a virtual stranger, could find her, then so could her father. He was a very powerful man. If he found out she was pregnant with his heir, she wouldn't stand a chance against him if he tried to take the baby from her.

"It wasn't hard," Ryder informed her. "The medicine bottle had a name on it and I had a friend check it out for me. It didn't take much to figure out who you were. It helped that you'd accessed your bank account here in Rocksprings."

Ryder didn't tell her that he still had the clippings announcing her marriage. Every time he looked at them he felt a little knot in his gut, but he hadn't been able to throw them away.

When he'd first read about it, he'd been shocked to find out that she'd spent what would have been her wedding night in his arms. Then he'd been just plain angry. What would make a woman run away on her wedding day and spend the night making love with a total stranger?

Surprised, Ashley stared at him. "How do you know that?"

"A friend did me a favor," he answered.

"Why did you bother?"

Ryder shook his head, and his chuckle sounded a little strangled. "I don't rightly know. That morning when I woke up and you were gone, I looked around and there was nothing of yours left in the room. I had to convince myself that you weren't a figment of my imagination. To tell you the truth, at first I thought you'd rolled me."

"I wouldn't have done that." Ashley smiled a little at the thought.

"I know that now, but I had a few choice words for you at the time. Then I guess when I figured out you hadn't taken my wallet, it made me wonder why you'd given yourself to me that night. Were you just out for a one-night stand?"

"Of course not!" Ashley stated indignantly. "I'd never done anything like that in my life." She blushed when she looked into his eyes.

"Yeah, I could tell," Ryder answered, and his knowing look left no doubt as to how. "Then why did you leave that morning?"

Ashley sighed heavily. "I panicked. I couldn't believe I'd done something so irresponsible." So irresponsible that she'd gotten pregnant. Her thoughts made every muscle, every nerve in her body tense.

She just couldn't tell him about the baby. This baby was her chance to start over. Maybe she didn't have the kind of money she was raised with, but that didn't mean she couldn't take care of herself. She'd have a chance to live her life her own way. And she wanted this baby.

What if he found out and tried to take it away from her? She couldn't stop the feeling of pure terror that rose inside her. She wouldn't be able to stand it. No matter what, no one was going to raise her child but her.

"Why did you?" Ryder asked bluntly. "I know something, or better, someone, had made you upset enough to take pills. I thought when you woke up in the middle of the night that they'd worn off and you knew what you were doing."

"I did," Ashley admitted honestly. Those hours in his arms had taught her more about life than she'd ever been allowed to learn on her own. But what she'd done wasn't anything to be proud of, either. "As I said before, I'd had a shock earlier and I was running on pure adrenaline. I needed someone, and you just happened to be there for me."

Ryder grimaced. "Anyone would have done," he concluded, a frown creasing his forehead. "Is that right?"

Ashley didn't deny his accusation. If he thought the night she'd spent with him meant nothing special to her, he'd probably leave her alone—which was exactly what she wanted. She was afraid of what he could make her feel and just as afraid of him finding out about the baby.

Feeling as though he'd been struck, Ryder stared at Ashley. He'd always thought of himself as a good judge of character. At least he had been before he'd met Ariel. Ashley was no different, he was finding out. Feeling gullible left a bad taste in his mouth.

Gritting his teeth, he said, "You haven't said why you were

there in the first place. What was so shocking that you ended up alone in the Blue Eagle?'' he asked.

Ashley's spine stiffened. "That's not important now."

"Maybe not to you, but it is to me. Was it your family?" he pressed.

Her eyes flew to his. "What makes you ask that?"

He shrugged. "Once I found out who your father was, I started wondering if the way you acted had anything to do with him. A lot of people who grow up in privileged households have a difficult time adjusting to life." His tone was matter-of-fact.

"You think I was a spoiled little rich girl out to defy my parents because I couldn't have my own way," she surmised. Ashley supposed that would have been a logical conclusion. But he couldn't have been more wrong. She was too embarrassed to admit how she was raised. In a way, it *was* defiance that drove her to take off on her own.

"You wouldn't be the first," Ryder told her. "That's exactly what I thought when I first laid eyes on you." Then, after he'd rescued her, she'd looked at him so innocently, he'd been foolish enough to believe he was wrong. Well, she'd proved just the opposite by her actions.

"That wasn't the way it was." She touched his arm, then snatched her hand back when she felt his corded muscles tighten. "Really, it wasn't."

"What was it, then, Ashley?" he asked, not really believing her.

Ashley stood and walked away, then turned to face him. She folded her arms about her. "Look this is getting us nowhere. Why I did what I did isn't really important. It happened. It's over. Let's just put it behind us."

Ryder stood and approached her. "What if I don't choose to do that?" he asked, goading her. He still had a feeling that she wasn't being quite truthful. He wanted to know why.

"You don't have that option."

"I say I do." He stepped closer, leaving only inches between them. "No matter what you say, there's still some spark between us. You can deny it all you want. It won't make it go away.'' That he wanted her wasn't debatable. He'd wanted her from the first moment he'd walked into the diner and he still wanted her now. Being near her was making him damned uncomfortable.

Cupping his hand behind her head, he drew her closer. She put a hand against his chest, but he lowered his head and very slowly, very deliberately, touched his mouth to hers. He kissed first one corner, then the other. She tasted soft and just as innocent as he remembered.

Then he took her mouth fully and ran his tongue along her lips, sucking gently on them, coaxing them open. His tongue slipped past her teeth into the warmth of her mouth, then withdrew. So sweet, so good. Everything he'd been unable to forget. Her taste, her smell, the feel of her mouth beneath his. So damn sweet.

Soon the kiss turned into something more, something Ashley seemed unable to control. Ryder's hand on her neck held her to him and her palm went to his cheek. She made a soft, sensual sound in her throat as she accepted the rough caress of his tongue.

The languid heat that stole through Ashley jarred her senses and a slow-burning coal of fire heated her belly. She forgot everything but the way this man made her feel.

Wanted.

Needed.

He'd made her feel that way once before and she'd ended up sleeping with him. He made her feel all the things she'd longed for when she was growing up. For a few heady minutes she leaned closer to him, seeking his warmth, the hardness of his body, any part of him, every part of him.

He seemed to fill her, touch something deep inside her that she kept hidden away. There was something so right about being held by him. Ashley felt his body shudder when she slid her arms around his neck, her fingers toying with the blond strands of his hair. His hands went to her waist, pulling her closer into the heat of his embrace.

Ryder's hand slid up her rib cage to her breast and he touched her, finding her hardened nipple through the soft fabric of her blouse. Ashley gasped from the intimate contact of his caressing fingers. She drew away from him and pushed hard against his chest, aware of the thunderous beat of his heart as she opened her eyes and stared at him.

"Stop, please," she cried, her voice whisper soft. She tried to push away from him, but Ryder's firm grip kept her from moving.

"Ashley," he began, only to be cut off when she shook her head and spoke.

"No, I can't. I won't." Her eyes speared him, shimmering with unshed tears. She didn't want to get involved with him any more than she was. She'd learned the hard way not to trust men and had no reason to trust this one. She couldn't take a chance on him trying to take her child from her. "I'm not going to sleep with you again." There was a desperate note to her voice.

For a moment Ryder just glared at her, his lips pressed tight. He took a deep breath and expelled it with a long sigh, as if his patience was being sorely tested. "I'm not asking you to."

Ashley knew that wasn't true. He hadn't said the words, but his body, his kisses, his touch, had made his intentions perfectly clear. Her own body had clamored for the same wild release. But she couldn't afford to give in to those feelings.

"Ryder, I just don't want to get involved with you. I think you'd better go." Ashley felt a sense of connection with this man that scared her. She told herself it was just because he was her baby's father. She didn't need him or want him in her life.

Ryder frowned. "Darlin', we're already involved up to our eyeballs. If you think we're not, just remember how easily we go up in flames every time we touch." His thumb grazed her lower lip, still swollen from his kisses.

"That's just—"

"Sex?" he interjected, repeating what she'd said earlier at the diner. "Maybe so. Why don't we just go with it and see where it takes us?'' He stroked a hand across her shoulder and down her arm.

Ashley pushed against his chest and was relieved when he turned her loose. She retreated to the far edge of the porch, a safe haven if only a small distance away from him. ''I don't think that's a good idea.'' The desire smoldering in his eyes told her exactly where it would lead if she spent *any* time with him.

''All right. I'll go and give you some space. But make no mistake about it, darlin'. I'll be back.''

Ashley shook her head. ''No.''

''Yes, Ashley.'' The stubborn remark was gentled by the softness in his blue eyes.

''I want you to leave me alone.''

''I'm not ready to do that.''

''Why?'' she asked, her gaze desperately searching his expression. ''Why can't you just leave me alone? What is it you want from me?''

''I don't know.'' Ryder wasn't sure what to say because he wasn't sure of his own motives. He knew he wanted her in the most basic way, felt she wanted the same thing, despite her protests. She intrigued him, and he'd never been intrigued by a woman in his life. Nor had he wanted a woman more than he wanted her. Not even Ariel. That thought scared him, but not enough to make him walk away just yet.

He still wanted some answers. He wanted to know who Ashley Bennett was, why she'd slept with him on her wedding day and why she was so evasive.

Grabbing his hat, he jammed it on his head. ''I'll see you in the morning.'' Before she could say another word, he went down the porch steps and walked away.

Ashley watched him adjust his hat on his head as he walked up the street, his stride easy. The man just didn't seem to know the word *no*. Well, he was going to learn, even if it meant the hard way. Ashley was determined to take care of her own problems.

So far no one in her family had come looking for her. But

Ryder could have unknowingly stirred up trouble for her by asking questions about her. Damn Ryder McCall for giving her yet another thing to worry about. Ashley wanted to stand on her own two feet. Maybe she'd never wanted for money, but she was working hard now and earning her own way. It felt good that she could take care of herself and her child.

Miss Tilley was already gone the next morning when Ashley awoke. Hopefully, by the time she returned, Ryder would be out of her life. Bess, however, was full of questions when Ashley arrived at the diner an hour later.

"Everything go okay last night?" She started several pots of coffee brewing.

"Not exactly," Ashley answered, reaching for a clean apron and tying it around her slightly thickening waist.

"You feelin' poorly again this morning?" Bess looked up from her task and searched Ashley's ashen face.

"A little." She tried to smile reassuringly, hoping that the morning sickness would pass quickly. "I'm fine. Really."

Her expression full of concern, Bess asked bluntly, "Is Ryder the baby's father?"

Ashley had told Bess of her broken engagement when she'd first asked for the job as waitress. She'd explained that she needed some time alone to think about what she wanted to do with her life. Several weeks later when she realized she was pregnant, she'd told Bess that, too.

"Yes." Ashley looked away and busied her hands by filling salt and pepper shakers.

Bess turned on the grill and tossed a large slab of bacon on it. "From what I can tell, he seems like a nice enough fella. Why didn't you want to marry him?"

Ashley's hands stilled. "Oh, Bess," she murmured, looking away. Tears filled her eyes. At that moment, she felt as if the weight of the world was on her shoulders. "I don't know how to tell you this."

Bess turned the heat down on the grill and walked over.

She gently patted Ashley's back. "What is it, child?" she asked, worry etched in the lines of her craggy face.

Ashley met Bess's eyes, her expression somber. "What I have to tell you, well, I just don't want you to think bad of me."

Bess hugged her. "Nothing you could say would make me change the way I feel about you, child. You must know that."

Ashley didn't know how to say it tactfully, so she just blurted out, "Ryder isn't the man I was engaged to. He's the baby's father, but I only spent one night with him. The night before I showed up here." She expected to see shock and disappointment register on Bess's face, but she didn't.

Ashley quickly explained that she'd left home when she'd found her fiancé with another woman on her wedding day. "I did some foolish things that night, one of them was going to bed with a stranger."

"Ryder."

Ashley compressed her lips and swallowed hard. "Yes." She filled in the rest of the details, how she'd been sick, how Ryder had taken care of her. "He never once made a pass at me. I was the one who encouraged him." She flushed but continued talking. "I needed something that night and Ryder seemed to be able to give it to me.

"I'm not talking about sex. It probably sounds stupid, but it was much more than that. You see, my stepmother is a cold woman and my father, well, from the time I was born, he forgot I existed. The only thing he cares about is money. I was never shown love or approval. No one ever held me or tucked me in bed at night."

Drawing a breath, she sniffed back tears. To give her hands something to do, she began filling the shakers again as she talked. "That night I woke up to find Ryder sleeping beside me." Her hands shook and she took a deep breath to calm herself. "He'd stayed with me through the night just to be sure I was all right. He was gentle and kind and treated me special. I just wanted one perfect memory, one time in my life when someone wasn't controlling or using me."

Bess picked up the spatula and turned her attention to the grill, spreading the bacon out, watching it pop and sizzle. "I guess you never intended to turn up pregnant, either, did you?"

"No, I didn't." Ashley blushed bloodred. "Even now, I can't believe how irresponsible I was."

"So I guess you haven't thought much about him since then?"

Ashley wanted to lie but she couldn't. She *had* thought about Ryder. Too often. But she'd told herself that a man like Ryder McCall had probably slept with a lot of women. She'd been just a warm body in the night. That was all.

"If you have to think about your answer that long, I guess I can figure it out. 'Course, it don't surprise me none. The man oozes sex appeal."

Ashley's head whipped around. "Bess!" Keeping herself from grinning, she forced a frown.

"I might be an old married woman, but I've still got eyes. It doesn't hurt to look, and your man's real easy on the eyes."

"He's not my man," Ashley quickly replied, scowling.

"So you weren't going to search him out and tell him he was going to be a father?"

"No," Ashley admitted, and felt her cheeks burn from the admission. "It's my responsibility. I got myself into this. Anyway, I'll never be sorry about the baby."

"Ashley, child, it took both of you to make that baby. That makes it half his. Besides, whether you want to tell him or not is irrelevant. I don't think you're going to have any choice."

"What do you mean?" Ashley looked up at Bess, who nodded toward the front window of the diner.

"Look outside."

Ashley's gaze followed Bess's and she saw Ryder stop his truck in front of the diner. Seconds later he came strolling in as if he'd been doing it for years. He stopped just on the other side of the counter.

"Morning," he said as he looked at Ashley. His gaze took

in her frown and pale skin color. "Are you feeling all right?"
he asked.

"Yes. Of course," she insisted, wishing everyone would
stop asking her that.

Ryder's gaze flickered to Bess. "Ma'am," he drawled, nodding at her. Since he was the first customer, he took the booth
he'd had the day before.

"What can I get you?" Ashley had followed him and
waited by his table for his order, silently wondering what she
was going to do. She had to get rid of him. If he hung around
too long, he'd soon find out he was going to be a father. She
couldn't risk that.

Ryder didn't even look at the menu. "A big breakfast. Pan-
cakes would be nice. You decide what to bring with them,"
he answered, still smiling. "And coffee, black—"

"No sugar. Right," she replied, then could have smacked
herself. She didn't want him to think she paid particular attention to his habits. Flushing, she rushed on, "I have an ex-
cellent memory."

Blue eyes met dark brown ones and suddenly it seemed as
if they were alone in the room. Somewhere in the distance,
Ashley heard the bells over the door jingle as other customers
came in, but her gaze seemed to be glued to Ryder.

His voice was low when he spoke. "Good. That means you
haven't forgotten."

Feeling as if she were under hypnosis, she asked, "Forgotten what?"

Ryder took hold of her hand and rubbed his thumb over the
pulse point of her wrist. "What it was like between us that
night. What it felt like when I touched you, when you touched
me."

Ashley wet her lips. God, she didn't want to remember, but
she hadn't been able to forget. "Ryder," she whispered. She'd
meant it to sound like a warning, but it came out more like a
moan. She couldn't let him do this to her. She turned and
quickly walked away, eager to get herself on sure footing once
again.

Fascinated by her body, Ryder watched Ashley hurry away from him. Several people had come into the diner, which seemed to be a popular morning spot. Ryder continued to watch Ashley as she worked. She had a good rapport with the customers, both the men and the women. In the short amount of time she'd been here, it seemed she was really well liked.

Well, Ryder could understand that. There was a lot to like about her. Today she was dressed once again in jeans, which encased her derriere and hugged her thighs. The sleeveless shirt she wore with them was white and had an open collar. She'd braided her dark hair in some sort of twist that made it look shorter than it was, but it was really pretty.

His eyes skimmed hungrily over her. She'd changed a lot in the past months. That night in the bar she'd reeked of class and high society. Now she looked as if she could have come from any one of the nearby farms or ranches.

She still looked mighty young. Ryder grimaced. Her age had given him more than one nightmare since the night he'd spent with her. He didn't need Jacob Bennett coming after him with a shotgun. Since she'd been about to get married, he'd assumed she was over eighteen. If she wasn't, he could be in a heck of a lot of trouble.

The door to the diner opened, and Ryder's gaze shifted to the man who walked in. He was tall and of medium build, well-muscled and looked somewhere around his brother Jake's age, which was thirty-two. Dressed in a khaki uniform, he had a badge pinned on his shirt and a lethal looking gun strapped to his hip.

Ryder didn't have to guess who he was. The sheriff in the flesh. Ryder watched him move through the room, his gaze resting for a split second on Ryder before he continued on.

Apparently the sheriff missed nothing. Ryder gritted his teeth when the man took a seat at the counter and called out to Ashley. She turned and smiled, her eyes softening as she spoke to him. Ryder had the sudden urge to go over and sock the sheriff square in the jaw, then told himself to calm down.

Punching out the sheriff wouldn't do a thing but land him in jail.

Ashley seemed to remember Ryder was there, because her gaze locked briefly with his before going back to the sheriff. When Ryder saw the sheriff reach for Ashley's hand, he wondered again just how friendly they were.

Ryder slid deeper into the seat and settled back, trying his best to look nonchalant while every single muscle in his body tensed. Maybe that's why Ashley wanted him to leave her alone. Maybe she hadn't told him the truth and had something going with the sheriff.

He released a pent-up breath when Ashley withdrew her hand and poured coffee into the sheriff's cup. Ryder noticed her hand shook a bit. He wished he could attribute that to his presence and not the other man's. Ryder wanted to be the one to make Ashley tremble. He wanted to make Ashley remember how it had been between them.

Trouble was, Ashley kept insisting she wanted to be left alone. Still, there were some answers he wanted and he was going to get them...whether she liked it or not.

She came back to Ryder's table long enough to set his breakfast in front of him. It seemed to Ryder that she took great pains to keep her distance. Her eyes guarded, she made sure he had everything he'd asked for without really looking at him. Then she took off again as quickly as she could. For a while Ryder had to be satisfied with watching her wait on the other customers that came in for breakfast.

While he was eating, Ryder caught a speculative look or two from the sheriff. From anyone else, he would have assumed the cursory glances were nothing more than curiosity about a stranger passing through the town. Instead, because it was the sheriff doing the looking, he felt as if he were being sized up.

He evened up the score by checking out the sheriff as he finished his meal. He seemed relaxed as he sipped his mug of coffee, yet Ryder wasn't fooled. There was a tenseness about him, a quiet sense of awareness. It showed in the way his shoulders never loosened and in the alert look in his eyes. And Ryder didn't like the way the sheriff never quite took his eyes off Ashley.

Ryder, too, was aware of every move Ashley made, which included each time she spoke to the sheriff, each smile she sent his way, the soft look that came into her eyes when she spoke to him. A spark of jealousy stirred deep inside Ryder, which surprised him, because he'd vowed never to care that much about another woman. Ariel had done a job on his heart. No other woman was going to get the chance to humiliate him again. But wanting Ashley Bennett didn't mean he wanted to spend his life with her. No way.

Ryder had made himself content to run the ranch with his brothers and sister. His family meant everything to him. They'd stood beside him when Ariel had made a laughing-stock of him, when everyone in the county had heard what a fool he'd been.

He was drawn from his reflecting when Ashley approached his table. She didn't look at him as she worked her pencil across the tablet, then ripped off a page and placed it on his table.

Six

"Join me for a few minutes," Ryder said quietly.

"I'm working. I don't have time." Ashley had done her best to stay as far away from him as possible, to avoid any chance of physical contact. It was true she was attracted to him; there was no way she could deny it to herself. What galled her was that apparently it was obvious to him.

Ryder's gaze surveyed the diner. The breakfast rush was definitely behind her. The only customers remaining were a young couple at a booth and the sheriff, who hadn't so much as budged since he'd walked in the door.

"You can give me a few minutes. Sit." He wasn't giving her a choice. She could sit in the booth with him or he'd personally put her there. His expression told her as much. He grasped her hand and tugged until she finally slid onto the seat across from him, her shoulders tensed as if preparing for battle.

"Stop manhandling me," she snapped, glaring at the grip he had on her. Just as she feared, his touch was doing wild things to her, making every single nerve ending along her skin tingle with excitement. She fought the delicious sensations and frowned.

Ryder easily read her expression and wanted to chuckle, but thought better of it. Still, he didn't let go. "I wouldn't have to if you didn't ignore me."

"I wasn't ignoring you," she protested, her dark eyes shooting sparks at him. "Unlike you, I was working. Don't you have a job to do or something?" Though he'd said his family owned a ranch, he looked like a man who worked hard for a living. His shoulders were broad and hard-muscled and his big hands were callused. Surely his family was missing him by now.

"Sure I work," Ryder assured her, a disarming smile curving his lips. "I've just finished negotiating the sale of some horses for the ranch. I was on my way home when I came to see you."

Ashley glared again. "Well, don't let me hold you up." She pulled at her hand again, but he held on to her.

"Is there a problem here?"

Both of them turned toward the person intruding on their conversation. Ryder wasn't really surprised to find the sheriff standing beside the table. He'd been keeping his eye on him for the past few minutes and was aware they had captured his attention. Up close, the man exuded a presence of determination and will...and authority. Ryder didn't want to tangle with him, but he would if it came down to it.

"No problem that I can see, Sheriff." Loosening his grip on her somewhat, his gaze flickered to Ashley. "We're just having a private discussion."

The sheriff's gaze shifted to Ashley, and the harsh look in his eyes gentled as he lifted an eyebrow. "Ashley?"

"It's all right, Slade." She took advantage of Ryder's relaxed hold to remove her hand from his grasp, which afforded her a sharp look from him. "This is an acquaintance of mine, Ryder McCall."

Acquaintance. Damn it all to hell, Ryder thought, there was that word again. It was beginning to grate on his nerves.

"Acquaintance," he repeated, then gave Ashley a smile chock-full of charm, the look in his eyes beaming with mischief. "That's real cute, darlin', considering how well acquainted we are."

"Ryder." She sent him a blistering look.

His expression was one of unabashed innocence as he added, "I'm only speaking the truth." Very deliberately he raised his head and met the speculative look in the sheriff's eyes. "There's not another man on earth that knows Ashley as well as I do."

Fuming, Ashley reared her foot back and kicked Ryder's shin as hard as she could.

"Ouch!" Ryder growled, then reached under the table and kneaded his leg with his hand. He looked at Ashley, and she was smiling sweetly.

"So help me, Ryder McCall, if you don't behave I'll borrow the sheriff's gun and shoot you." She looked up at Slade and smiled sweetly.

He shifted his stance and appeared to relax a little.

"Well, if you're sure you're okay." He didn't exactly sound convinced. "You know where to find me if you need me." His last words were spoken with a warning glance at Ryder.

"Thank you, Slade."

Ryder was still scowling as the sheriff walked out the door. "Dammit, what was that for?"

"You know *exactly* what it was for. How dare you imply there's something between us?"

Ryder straightened and glared at her. "It's the truth," he answered obstinately.

"Only in your mind." She got out of the booth, and Ryder followed, detaining her by pinning her between him and the table.

"Like hell."

Ashley wanted to move away from him, but there was nowhere to go. Her rear was pressed against the table, and she braced her hands against its edge, trying to overcome the spark of awareness that shot through her.

"Why can't you just leave me alone?"

Ryder leaned closer to her, so close that there was barely breathing space between them. "Because we have some unfinished business. You know it and I know it and the sooner you admit as much, we can get on with it."

His mouth was only a breath away from hers. His lids slid halfway over his blue eyes, dropping his gaze to her mouth. His lips hovered, his breath tantalizing hers as she breathed in the very essence of him.

Ashley knew he was going to kiss her, and despite her resolve, she held her breath in anticipation. Never before had a man affected her like this cowboy. She placed her hands against his chest as if to hold him off, though aware that she ached to pull him closer.

"Ryder—" She clenched her hands in his shirt.

"I still want some answers," he insisted. "When you've told me everything I want to know, I'll leave if you still want me to," he whispered, his breath fanning her ear. His tongue slipped out to caress it and his teeth nibbled her lobe. To anyone else in the room, it would appear he was merely whispering to her.

Ashley knew she had only to move her head just slightly and her lips would meet his. Ryder reached behind her, which drew him closer still. She closed her eyes and lifted her face, aching for the contact of his mouth on hers.

His lips touched her lips briefly, then they were gone. The fleeting contact was so unexpected, Ashley opened her eyes in surprise. To her chagrin, he was adjusting his hat on his head. He tilted it just so, then winked at her.

Ashley's face reddened.

Ryder looked at her stunned expression, her flushed face and the sultry look of desire in her eyes. "As I said, darlin', we've got unfinished business between us. I'll pick you up at seven sharp."

Before she could answer, he turned and strode out the door. It took a moment for her to realize he'd teased her on purpose, just to prove some sort of macho point. It was a good thing he was gone. If he had still been standing in front of her, she'd have crowned him with his breakfast plate!

She glanced at the remaining occupants of the diner, and they quickly averted their eyes. Hurrying to the kitchen, she began cleaning the dishes.

Ashley spent the rest of the day working hard and trying to forget Ryder McCall. Try as she might, it was just too impossible a task.

The night she'd spent with him had taught her a lot about him. He was compassionate and kind. He'd taken care of her when he could have left her alone and sick. His family meant a lot to him. She could see the love he had for them in his eyes when he spoke of them. She shook her head. He was also tenacious when he was after something. To her, that spelled trouble.

At closing time Ashley was alone in the diner. Bess had left earlier, having received a call from home that her youngest boy was sick. Ashley locked the diner door, then looked both ways down the road. Ryder was nowhere in sight.

"Well, doesn't that just beat all," she said to herself, annoyed that deep down she felt the slightest bit disappointed. Here she'd spent the entire day worrying over seeing him again, and he'd stood her up. Relief washed through her as she reminded herself that her goal was to get rid of him. Apparently she'd accomplished that.

She started toward Miss Tilley's but had gone no further than a block when she heard the sound of an engine winding down. Without moving her head, she darted her eyes to the street and recognized Ryder's black, dust-covered truck. Ignoring him, she continued to walk.

"C'mon, darlin, hop in," he called through the open window. His coaxing tone was carried to her on a soft summer breeze.

Ashley kept the same pace and tried her best not to respond to his cheerful mood. She wasn't at his beck and call. She'd never agreed to meet him. Sooner or later he would learn he couldn't just tell her what to do.

"Ashley," he called again, some of the patience now absent from his voice.

When she didn't respond, he sped on up ahead of her. She watched him pull to the side of the road, his tires skidding on the rocks as his brakes jammed.

Ryder quickly got out, leaving the door open behind him and the engine idling. He came around the back of the truck just as she was approaching. Ashley started to cross the street, but he blocked her path with his body.

"Oh, no, you don't." He grabbed her shoulders and held her still. She tried to shrug off his hands.

"Get out of my way."

"Get in the truck."

"No." She stared up at him, unblinking, her chin tilted at a stubborn angle.

"All right."

Before Ashley could breath a sigh of relief, Ryder bent down and scooped her up in his arms. He stalked over to the truck and deposited her inside. Ashley promptly scooted to the other side of the seat and reached for the passenger door handle. As she tried to grasp it, Ryder got in the truck and hauled her back to his side.

"Let me out of this truck this minute!"

"Not on your life, darlin'." Ryder shifted the gears and made a swift U-turn, then picked up speed as he headed out of town.

"Where are you taking me?" Ashley demanded.

"To dinner," he answered without elaborating.

"I don't want to go to dinner with you."

Ryder shot her a hard look. "I figured that much out when you refused to get in the truck."

"Look, you can't arrange my life to suit you," she insisted, her gaze boiling. Ryder remained silent, his attention on the road. "Ryder, I mean it. Turn this truck around." She paused, then added firmly, "Now." Her tone was adamant and forced him to look at her.

"What could having dinner hurt? After we talk things over,

I'll leave you alone if you want." It was becoming apparent that she didn't want anything to do with him. If she continued to persist, he'd give her what she wanted. Hell, there were plenty of other women out there. He didn't have to have this one.

"If I go to dinner with you, you'll leave me alone?" Ashley asked, sounding distrustful. She didn't want any contact with him. The less she saw of him, the better. If he walked out of her life, maybe she wouldn't feel so guilty about keeping the baby a secret.

To be truthful to herself, it was getting harder and harder to say no to him. What was wrong with her? Why did she feel as if this man had the power to fill some need in her? It was the same strong feeling she'd experienced the night they'd spent together.

Gritting her teeth, she looked away from him, determined to remain aloof. She couldn't let him get too close. There was the baby to think about.

That was something she *had* to keep from him. No one was going to intrude in her life any longer, make decisions for her, tell her what to do. She'd had enough of that; she wasn't going to take it anymore.

"This is kidnapping, you know."

Ryder shot her a speaking glance, then returned his eyes to the road, watching for the restaurant he'd spotted earlier on his way back from the ranch. The quiet stretched out between them until it felt like a band of steel about to snap under pressure.

She'd made it plain she wanted nothing more to do with him. That irritated the hell out him. He'd spent the night with her, made love with her until he was worn out from the pleasure of it, and she wanted him to leave her alone. Hell, to her he'd been a one-night stand.

He took Route 277 and headed for Sonora, where he eventually turned into the driveway of a quaint restaurant on the outskirts of town.

"Have you been here before?" he asked conversationally.

Ashley shook her head, then tucked a loose strand of hair back into her braid. "I haven't been out of Rocksprings since the day I arrived." She didn't admit it, but she'd avoided going anywhere near Sonora where she'd first met him. She hadn't wanted to chance running into him.

"Then let's investigate this place and see if the prime rib is as good as they claim." He got out of the truck and shut the door.

Ashley didn't wait for him to get her door. She got out and met him in front of the truck.

Inside, the restaurant was busy, but not noisy. The hostess seated them in a booth in the back. Ashley sat across from him, needing the distance the table provided. The waitress stopped by their table and offered to take their drink order.

Ryder ordered a beer, then looked to Ashley for her request.

"Iced tea," she told the waitress.

Ryder smiled, then ordered an iced tea along with his beer. The waitress gave them menus and left.

"Abstaining from alcohol," he commented with a smile, unable to resist teasing her a bit.

"After what happened last time, I don't care if I ever drink alcohol again," Ashley confessed, her face heating.

Ryder sobered, taking her barb personally. "It wasn't all bad, was it?"

"No." Ashley didn't want him to think that she hated him. After all, she'd been the aggressor that night, not Ryder. But she didn't want him to know how good he'd made her feel, either.

"Thank you for that," Ryder replied, though he took little solace from her words. It was clear that she wanted him out of her life. But nagging at the back of his mind was how she'd responded when he'd kissed her earlier. He sat back in his seat and looked at her. "Are you ready to tell me what happened?"

"I don't know why it's so important for you to know," she answered, "but if that's what it'll take to satisfy you, well…" She shrugged and was silent a moment.

"That's hardly what it'll take to satisfy me," Ryder told her. He raised an eyebrow, his expression suggestive.

Ashley ignored his innuendo. "You know my name and who my father is."

Ryder nodded. "I've heard he's a tough old bastard," he said bluntly. He'd never done business with the man, but had heard from business acquaintances that Jacob Bennett was a hard-as-nails businessman who took a hell of a lot more than he gave.

Ashley's lips tightened. "That's putting it nicely. I once heard him say that he'd only had a child because my mother begged him, and then he'd resented the fact that I was a girl. He never had very much to do with me. Then my mother died, and within a year he remarried. I never really got along with my stepmother, Iris."

"Was it the typical jealousy kids usually feel when a parent remarries?"

She shook her head. "I don't know. I was only six. I thought that my mother had left me because she didn't love me. I didn't understand what dying meant. No one ever talked to me about it. Then all of a sudden I had a stepmother." She sighed, then started fiddling with her place setting.

"She wasn't loving like my mother had been. She never hugged me or told me she loved me. She was a very cold woman, very demanding, and I couldn't seem to do anything to please her. She made me take dancing lessons, but I wasn't very good. I had to take piano. I hated it, but she made me practice for hours every day. When other kids were out playing with friends, I was kept inside. She seemed to take pleasure in telling me what a disappointment I was to her and my father."

"And you believed her."

"Yes. I never had a reason to believe otherwise." She sighed softly, then continued. "My father was never home. Working, making money, was the only thing he cared about. I'm sure he only remarried so he wouldn't have to care for me." She looked away in an effort to gather her resolve. She didn't want to care about the fact that her father didn't love her, resented the fact that she did. Baring her soul was humiliating enough without seeing pity in Ryder's eyes.

"I can't imagine growing up like that," Ryder commented, thinking how hard it must have been for her. She'd grown up without love, without happiness. She'd thought her own mother had left her because she wasn't worthy of loving.

"Not all families are like that," he told her, wanting her to know it wasn't *her*, that she'd had nothing to do with how she was raised. "My parents were just the opposite. They'd loved and nurtured us, made us their whole life." He looked in her eyes and saw her pain. "It must have been hard to deal with."

"It was. As I got older, Iris's demands were even tougher. I couldn't seem to please her in any way. I had to study all the time to try and make good grades. Even though I always made honor reports, they weren't even good enough for her." Ashley shook her head, her expression bitter. "All she did was berate me and accuse me of not trying hard enough to make straight As."

She paused when the waitress came to take their order. After the young woman left, Ashley continued, "She disapproved of socializing, would never let me have a friend over or let me spend the night out. She didn't even trust me to go to the shopping mall on my own. I felt like I lived in a prison."

"You didn't rebel?"

Ashley's laugh wasn't humorous. "Oh, sure I did. But I learned that if I wanted to eat, I'd better do exactly what she wanted." She'd been locked in her room more than once. She shivered from the memory, then thought of the baby growing inside her. Because she'd been brought up by a mean and hurtful parent, Ashley was determined to be the best mother to her own child. Maybe it wouldn't have a mother and a father, but she would give it plenty of love. And she would have someone to love her back.

"I'm sorry. I sort of got off track." She cleared her mind of what she was thinking and went on. "I learned the behavior that kept me out of trouble with her. I didn't really see a way out of living there. She wouldn't let me go to college or get a job. She wanted me to marry someone in my *class,* someone worthy of the Bennett name. That's when I met Martin, the man I was engaged to.''

She stopped speaking when the waitress brought their food. She hadn't realized she was hungry until it was put before her. She'd had a few crackers that morning to combat the morning sickness and nothing much else.

Ryder wondered again what part her fiancé played in her life. Obviously they hadn't been too close or she wouldn't have been a virgin on the night he'd met her. He wondered if she was still in love with him. Was it this Martin fellow she'd been thinking of when he'd been making love to her? He didn't like the thought of her with another man and damn well resented the fact that it bothered him.

''What happened after that?'' he prompted, needing to know why she'd spent her wedding night in his arms.

Ashley chewed the bite of food in her mouth and swallowed. It was hard to talk about Martin, but not because of her feelings for him. She felt exposed and humiliated. Taking a deep breath, she went on, wanting to get it over with.

''I thought he cared for me. Then I learned the night before I was going to marry him that he and my father had planned the entire courtship and marriage. It had something to do with this big merger between their corporations. Still, I decided to go through with it.'' She stuck her fork into a piece of meat while she stared at her plate. ''I saw marriage to him as a way out of having to live with Iris.'' She was ashamed to admit how desperate she'd been. She looked at Ryder to gauge his thoughts. His expression was serious, his eyes intent as he listened to her speak.

''Why didn't you go through with the marriage?''

Her stomach in knots, she'd lost what little appetite she'd had. She put her fork and knife across her plate. ''I found him in bed with someone else on our wedding day.'' Ashley swallowed past the lump in her throat and raised a hand to her cheek. Her face was warm, and she had to take another breath before she could go on.

"I was so shocked. I guess I was naive, too. Believing that he could really care about me." She'd learned not to expect love from anyone. She shouldn't have expected fidelity, either.

Tears burned her eyes, and Ashley hated herself for it. She was alone now, and she didn't need anyone's love or approval. "That was the last straw, all I could take." She sat back and looked away. "I took the coward's way out and left that morning and never went back."

Ryder reached over and laid his hand on hers. Though she didn't see it, it was a true test of her character that she'd had the courage to leave. "That was the night we met, the night at the Blue Eagle?" When she nodded, he drew in a deep breath. That was a hell of a lot for anyone to take.

"What about you?" she asked, diverting the conversation from the night they'd spent together. "Why haven't you ever married? Or are you the footloose and fancy-free type?" He was silent for a moment, as if contemplating his answer. Ashley noticed that his jaw clenched a fraction.

"Marriage isn't for everyone," he said quietly, thoughtfully. He stared across the room as if thinking, then admitted grimly, "I made the mistake of getting engaged once. It won't happen again."

"I take it that things didn't work out?" Ashley asked.

His laugh was bitter. "She was a real piece of work. She was sleeping around while we were together," he admitted blandly. "Then she ran off and married some old coot with money to burn."

Ashley couldn't believe any woman in her right mind would ever turn this man loose. "I'm sorry," she said, for lack of any other words of comfort she could offer.

"Don't be. Hell, it's the best thing that ever happened to me. I was never cut out for marriage and kids. I was lucky to get out of it."

Ashley let the subject drop and excused herself to go to the bathroom. Ryder watched her walk away, thinking that they both had a lot of emotional baggage. She was wary of men because of her father and the jerk she'd been engaged to. Ariel had taught him never to trust another woman. Ashley had grown up without a family's love, and though he'd had loving parents, he'd lost them at a very early age. Though a lot of years had passed, it still hurt when he thought of them.

Ryder figured that explained why they were so attracted to each other. Neither of them expected more than a warm body to be with for a while. Neither of them wanted to take a chance on getting emotionally involved.

He watched her as she headed back toward the table. She might not realize it, but she was tougher than she thought. Cutting herself off from the only support she'd ever had, well, it couldn't have been easy. But she'd done it and, from the way she looked, was taking pretty good care of herself.

Ashley returned to the table a few minutes later. She steered the conversation away from their personal lives and asked Ryder about his family. He told her about his younger sister, Lynn, who had just graduated from high school. He had an older brother, Jake, who had taken care of the family when their parents were killed. He didn't say what had happened to them and Ashley had the feeling it wasn't something he wanted to talk about.

Ashley was relieved when it was time to go. She'd felt tense when they'd first arrived, then during the evening, she'd actually enjoyed being with Ryder. He'd been easy to talk to, easy to be with.

She didn't want to like him. Because he would walk out of her life tonight, which was for the best. She could get on with her plans to raise her child alone.

Ryder led her to the truck, helped her inside, then went around and climbed behind the wheel. Their ride home was quiet, with neither of them saying much. When they arrived at Miss Tilley's house, Ryder walked her to the door and suggested she invite him in, insisting there were a couple more details he wanted cleared up.

Ashley acquiesced, telling herself she wouldn't have to see

him again after this night. She led him to the parlor and he sat one seat away from her on the floral print sofa.

"Where's Miss Tilley?" he asked, when it became obvious they were alone.

"Remember? She's visiting her sister for a couple of days." Ashley slipped off her shoes and tucked her feet beneath her, more to put a little distance between them than anything else. "Well, what else is it you want to know?" she asked. "I've pretty much bared my soul, so there isn't much left to wonder about."

Ryder shot her a look, then grinned, his straight white teeth showing just beneath his blond mustache. "How old are you?" he asked.

"You're kidding, right?"

He shook his head. "I'd like to know if I slept with a woman or a girl." He paused, eyeing her speculatively. "Are you over eighteen?"

Ashley laughed. "That's funny. One of the things I vaguely remember about that night was someone calling me jailbait. I was just too sick to say anything."

"That was Deke," Ryder told her.

Ashley nodded, a blurry vision of a younger Ryder passing through her mind. "Don't worry, no one is going to come after you with a shotgun. I'm twenty-two."

"Twenty-two!"

The relief that came over his expression was priceless, and Ashley laughed again. "You were really worried about that, weren't you?"

Ryder reached over and toyed with the strand of hair that had once again fallen free of her braid. "We didn't exactly do a lot of talking that night. I have to admit I've lost more than one night's sleep over your age."

"Well, you can relax, now that you know the truth." Ashley caught her breath at his sudden nearness. She told herself to pull away, but was drawn to him instead.

"It is a relief," he admitted. He moved a little closer to

her, close enough to ensnare her with his blue gaze. "There's something else," he said, and his voice held quiet concern.

"What?" Ashley asked, her tone a whisper. His nearness was doing strange things to her insides. He let go of her hair, then ran his fingers back and forth across her arm. Heat stole through her.

The silence of the house closed in on them, enveloping them in a cocoon of intimacy. Ashley wanted to move away, but she suddenly wanted his touch, also, as much as that first night she'd been with him. Torn, she remained still, her heart beating hard inside her chest.

"I'm ashamed to admit that I didn't protect you that night. I'm not usually so careless," he told her quickly. "You don't have to be afraid that I gave you anything."

Other than a baby. Ashley's stomach turned somersaults. Could she pull this off? she wondered. She knew by the way he'd talked about his fiancée that he didn't want any ties. He'd also said he didn't want children. To her way of thinking he'd validated her decision not to confess she was carrying his child.

"You know I couldn't have given you anything, either," she said, and held her breath.

"You gave me something pretty special," Ryder whispered, then leaned forward and touched his mouth to hers. He expected her to flinch and draw away, was surprised when she didn't. Her mouth was warm and tender. God, she was so sweet. Her taste, her smell, everything about her came at him at once, stirring him, making him want her even more.

He hadn't forgotten a thing about her. He wanted her naked against him, wanted to feel his body move into hers. His lips moved over hers, caressing them with infinite tenderness. She pulled slightly away, and their breaths mingled, their mouths barely apart.

"Ryder," she breathed out on a sigh. "Uh, this isn't a good idea," she protested weakly, obviously already as turned on as he was.

"It feels like a great idea," he whispered, planting kisses

strategically on her face before he touched his mouth to hers again.

Ashley knew an instant of hesitation before she gave in to his kiss. One more night. She'd take this one night with him, she rationalized. The damage had already been done. What difference could one night make now? her mind taunted.

"Ah, Ashley." Ryder deepened the kiss, slipping his tongue past her teeth to taste her fully. His hand moved to her rib cage and slid upward, stopping just short of her breasts.

"I remember what it was like between us that night, how good you felt in my arms, how it felt to be inside you. You've been like a taunting dream," he whispered when he lifted his mouth.

Ashley moaned as she leaned toward him and felt his mouth cover hers again. Her body was suddenly on fire. Her mind told her she had to stop this insanity, but she felt his tongue touch hers, and a need, basic and primal, snaked its way through her. Her hands went to his shoulders. Hard and strong, his muscles tensed beneath her touch.

Ryder kissed her deeply, his mouth hungry and searching. His hands went to her breasts and caressed them through the soft fabric of her cotton blouse. The buttons gave way as he opened them swiftly. He unclasped her bra, and her breasts flowed freely into his palms. His fingers caressed her, taking the hardened peaks between them.

Ashley was on fire. She arched and offered herself to him. Ryder kissed first one peak, then the other.

"Darlin', you're perfect, just like I remembered," he whispered. He tasted both mounds with his tongue, sucking one pebble-hard nipple, then the other, until her hips began to move rhythmically. His teeth nipped the tips of her breasts, and she moaned when he took her mouth once again.

Working furiously, Ashley quickly unbuttoned his shirt, exposing his muscular chest. She slid her hands over the expanse of it, then up to cup his neck as he kissed his way back to her breasts. When she went up on her knees, he began to unbuckle her jeans. He lowered her zipper, and then his hands slid inside to caress her bottom.

"Ryder," she cried, when the need for him became almost unbearable. Her voice seemed to excite him more. His fingers slid beneath her silk panties and touched the soft, innermost part of her. She arched against him, crying out his name again. Ashley felt him move away, but he was gone only long enough to rid himself of his clothes and boots.

He came back to her and removed her jeans, then slid her panties down her legs. Ready to explode, she caught her breath when he lowered her back to the sofa, then came down on her and slipped inside her with one swift thrust. Her hips arched as she took the length of him, and her breathing became labored and harsh.

Ryder set a pace that she felt compelled to follow. His mouth closed on hers and swallowed the sounds coming from her throat. His tongue moved in and out of her mouth, mimicking the part of him that filled the very core of her body.

Every nerve, every pore of her screamed for release. Ashley felt the spiral when it began uncoiling, spinning her out of control. The explosion inside her went on and on until she strained and her entire body tensed. Her hand clenched his shoulders, her fingers tightening as shudders of release ripped through her over and over again. Ryder must have felt her climax, for he plunged into her again and again, then trembled and called out her name.

Silence filled the room.

Their breathing ragged, neither said anything right away. The moment, quiet and soothing, wrapped around them. Ashley closed her eyes, savoring the feel of his body on hers, the closeness that she always seemed to crave when she was near this man. He began to move away and she whispered, "No."

Ryder slipped away from her, anyway. He drew a ragged breath as he got to his feet. A moment later he lifted her in his arms.

"Which way is your room?" he asked, securing her in his embrace.

"What?" she asked languidly, lifting her gaze to his.

"Which way?" he said again, already moving toward the stairs. He carried her to the top floor and through the door she indicated. He didn't stop to turn on the lights, but took her straight to the bed. Lowering her gently, he joined her, bringing her into his heat, his hands securing her against him.

The first thing he did was free her hair. He wanted to run his fingers through the silky strands. Facing her, he stroked her hair from her eyes so that he could watch the play of emotions that crossed her face. She was magnificent, her lips full and inviting, her eyes soft with desire. He slid his hand down her body, gliding it across her ribs, over the soft swell of her stomach, learning her all over again.

"You're so beautiful." He confessed his thoughts to her, amazed he could even speak.

"You make me feel beautiful," Ashley whispered. He filled the emptiness deep inside her, if only for a little while. Greedily she stole these moments with him, knowing she'd never see him again.

Ryder leaned over her and placed soft kisses on her mouth.

Their passion before had been so swift, so strong, he hadn't had time to explore her body. Now he wanted to take his time with her. Maybe if he made love to her again and again, his attraction would lessen and he could work her out of his system. Maybe, just maybe, he'd be able to walk away from her for good.

His hands moved to fondle her full breasts, tugging at her nipples, and she practically melted before his eyes. Her lids closed and she moaned softly, giving in to the delicious sensations he aroused when his palm slid down her body and stopped to stroke her soft triangle of curls. Her hips moved and she pushed upward toward his hand. His fingers slid lower then, slipping between the moist folds between her thighs. Her hips rocked back and forth in an age-old rhythm.

She whispered his name then, her voice soft, as the spark between them flared once again. Ryder bent his mouth to hers, his own passion out of control as he positioned himself and sank deep into her.

Seven

When Ryder woke, he was alone in Ashley's bed. Sunshine peeked through the lacy beige curtains on the windows. An instant replay of that long-ago morning ran through his mind, and he experienced a momentary sick feeling in his stomach before he heard the sound of running water coming from the nearby bathroom. It was ridiculous to think even for a moment that she'd taken off. Just because she'd done it that one time, didn't mean that she'd do it again.

Still...somewhere deep inside, he wasn't sure he really trusted her.

He raised his arm and rested it over his head and sighed contentedly as his body began to relax. They'd made love several times during the night and each time had been as exciting, as intense and consuming, as the first time he'd touched her. A wry smile curved his lips. No woman had ever moved him, become a part of him, as much as Ashley Bennett.

It scared him, letting her even that close. Ariel's betrayal had taught him he wasn't meant to settle down with a woman.

Emotionally, he had nothing to give Ashley Bennett, and he wasn't going to allow her any power over him. But just thinking about her made him hard, and he realized then that she could be more of a threat to him than Ariel had ever been.

He heard her moving around in the bathroom and thought she'd called out to him. Throwing the sheet off, he got out of bed and went downstairs in search of his clothes. He spotted his underwear and jeans beside the sofa and pulled them on. He picked up his shirt and went back upstairs, tossing it on a chair as he crossed to the bathroom door and knocked lightly.

"Ashley?" When she didn't answer, he frowned and called out, "You all right?"

"Yes. Leave me alone," she called from inside the room.

Ryder turned away, then he heard what sounded like gut-wrenching groans. Concerned, he opened the door and peeked inside the beige-tiled room. He saw Ashley on her knees on the vinyl floor, her head bent over the toilet, her hair covering her face.

"What the hell!" he exclaimed, then stormed into the bathroom.

"I said I'm all right. Go away," she moaned.

"All right? Darlin', I'd say you were anything but all right." He spotted a washcloth on the side of the small basin and wet it with cool water. He pressed it to Ashley's forehead, then grabbed most of her hair and held it back.

A small smile curved on his lips and he asked, "Darlin', does this only happen whenever you're around me?"

Ashley didn't see the humor of his words. Her head was swimming and her stomach felt like it had been ripped out of her and put back in sideways. And having the man you'd just spent the night loving find you with your head in the toilet was definitely the worst embarrassment a woman could suffer.

"Funny." She groaned, then started to get up.

Ryder slipped his arm around her. "Do you think you caught a bug?"

Knowing full well it was a lie, Ashley answered, "Probably.'' She let him help her from the room, then over to the edge of the bed.

"Thanks.''

Ryder eyed her speculatively. Her face was without color, her eyes shadowed. She'd slipped on a soft, off-white cotton gown. It covered her from shoulders to toes, but he could easily visualize what was underneath it. He knew her body well, had touched every inch of her.

"You don't look so good.''

Ashley lowered her head to her hands and covered her face. "Thanks again.'' She drew in a deep breath. When she'd fallen asleep in his arms, she hadn't given a thought about how she'd feel in the morning. How could she have been so stupid as to let him spend the night?

Ryder started to speak again when an errant thought jogged his memory. He closed his mouth and frowned. He remembered Miss Tilley mentioning that Ashley hadn't been feeling well lately. He also recalled that she hadn't looked so good the morning before when he'd gone to the diner to see her. Though, he rationalized, she'd seemed fine to him last night. He remembered stroking her, his hand slipping over her belly...

She was pregnant.

The thought hit him like a blow to his gut. No, she couldn't be. Ryder dismissed that explanation immediately, telling himself he was crazy. Ashley would have told him if that were so, wouldn't she?

Maybe not. She hadn't wanted him to hang around, had she? Was it possible that she'd known all along and deliberately kept it from him? For that matter, if it was true, was he even the father?

She raised her face, and Ryder immediately knew the truth when he looked into her hooded eyes.

"How long?'' Ryder asked tightly, shards of anger beginning to cut through him.

Ashley didn't even try to evade his hot blue gaze. "I've known for a while,'' she admitted, still sounding weak. Her stomach rolled and she clamped a hand over her mouth, holding her breath until the wave of nausea subsided.

Ryder's eyes bore into her. "Is it mine?"

Ashley threw her head back and straightened. Oh, God, she thought, did he have to ask? Did he think so little of her, believe that it was possible that she'd slept with another man so soon after being with him? "What do you think?" she answered, her voice stiff, the sarcasm in it unmistakable.

Ryder's lips twisted, anger pulsating through him like the vibrations of an earthquake, slowly building force until he thought he'd explode. He stalked away from her to the window and stared out at nothing. Turning to face her again, he said in a barely controlled tone, "I want to hear you say it. I want to hear you say that the baby's mine, that you've been hiding that fact from me since I came here, that you never intended to tell me."

He jammed his fingers into the back pockets of his jeans to keep from balling his fists and showing her just how near out of control he was. Her continued silence fueled his anger.

"Tell me the truth, dammit!" There was no gentleness in his voice, no endearing quality in his features. He was as angry with himself as he was with Ashley. He should have been more careful, should have used protection. For some reason, he didn't always think straight when he was around her.

Ashley flushed, turning red from the roots of her hair down to her throat and chest. "It's yours. I've never been with anyone else." The admission came grudgingly.

Ryder swore, and the words he used were not meant for virgin ears. In all his life, he'd never expected to be brought up short by something like this. He'd been responsible with women, hadn't been foolish enough to be with one without the benefit of protection since he was a teenager.

Until Ashley.

Hell.

He didn't even know how to react. A baby. What in the world did he know about babies, except that they were a hell of a lot of trouble.

"Were you even going to tell me?" he demanded, when he'd gained some sort of control over his temper.

Ashley stared at him in silence, then finally shook her head. "No," she answered honestly. What else could she say?

"That's a hell of an admission," he bit out, glaring at her.

She crossed her arms protectively over her stomach as she licked her lips, feeling nervous and jittery. "I'm sorry if it's not what you want to hear, but it's the truth. I know you're angry. But you weren't here. I didn't know where to find you. It didn't really matter to me, anyway. I'd already decided to raise the baby alone."

"What about what I might have wanted?" he grated. "Had you even given a thought about whether the baby would ever know me?"

"I assumed you weren't the type to settle down, and you even admitted as much to me last night. Since you don't want any ties, I thought it best not to involve you." She stood and reached for her robe, which was hanging in the closet beside the bed. She turned away to put it on, and her hands shook as she tied the sash.

"Well, I am involved. Hell, *we're* involved. Whenever I'm around you, we end up in bed."

Feeling flustered, Ashley ran her hand through her disheveled hair, brushing it from her face. He was right. She *was* physically attracted to him. Any chance of denying that ended when she'd made love with him again. Somehow, Ryder McCall had a way of getting past her barriers. But she couldn't let him jeopardize what she'd worked so hard for. "Well, I think it's best if we don't see each other again."

Ryder had a problem with that, but he let it go for the time being. "That's my baby, too," he declared. He wasn't thrilled about finding out he was going to be a father, but he damned well didn't like Ashley making all the decisions, as if he had no say in the matter.

Ashley swung around and faced him. "It's my body. Not yours. You don't *have* any rights when it comes to this baby."

Ashley saw his eyes harden to stone, their blue color turning nearly white with hot anger. She immediately wished she could call back her words.

Ryder bit back an oath and snarled, "Whether I like it or not, that baby in your body is a part of me, a part of my family. Don't you ever say that to me again, or I'll show you just how much influence I can have over you and that child."

His words went right to Ashley's heart and twisted it. She faced him squarely, though inside she was shaking like the aftershocks of an earthquake. "Don't you dare threaten me, Ryder McCall," she fumed, storming at him and stopping only about a foot away.

"Don't take it as a threat, darlin'." His tone harsh, his eyes blistering, Ryder looked right back at her without batting so much as an eyelash. "Take it as a fact. You don't want to tangle with me, sweetheart. You'd lose, I can promise you."

Ashley took a deep breath to calm her nerves. "This is getting us nowhere."

"You're right about that." Ryder stalked over and grabbed his shirt from the chair. He jerked it on, but left it unbuttoned. Turning to face her again, he raked her from head to toe with a harsh look. "Get dressed!" he commanded.

His demand startled her and her eyes widened. "What? Why?"

"Because I'm going to do the right thing and marry you."

Ashley's mouth dropped open, and a tremor of shock raced through her. That was the last thing she'd expected him to say. She didn't have to ask if he was serious—determination was written all over his face and in every movement of his body. The look she gave him was incredulous. "I'm not going to marry you!"

"The hell you're not," Ryder barked back at her.

"I'm *not* going to marry you," she repeated firmly, raising her voice a notch. "I don't *want* to marry you. I don't want to marry anybody." Heavens, how had she ever gotten into this mess?

"I'm not going to argue with you over this," Ryder told her, his tone furious and unbending.

"Well, that's good, because I don't want to argue with you over it." Ashley's hands went to her hips. She wasn't going to let him intimidate her.

"Dammit, Ashley—"

"Would you listen to yourself?" she interrupted, staring at him as if he were a madman. "This is the nineties. A woman doesn't have to get married to have a baby."

Ryder snorted. "Maybe not, but we're talking about my kid, and it's not going to be born illegitimate."

"That's ridiculous. Babies are born that way all the time," she argued.

"Not my baby and not a McCall," he snapped. "Now, whether you like it or not, we're going to get married and bring that baby into the world the right way."

"I don't want to get married," she said again.

Ryder growled, "That's beside the point."

"That's exactly the point. Neither of us wants to be married, to each other or anyone else. We don't even have anything in common."

Ryder looked pointedly at the bed, then back at her. "We've got the hots for each other. That's a start."

Exasperated, Ashley rolled her eyes. "That's ridiculous. You can't base a marriage on sex." He was being totally irrational.

"Well, at least if we're married, I'll know where in the hell you are and where my child is," Ryder stated hotly.

For a moment Ashley was too paralyzed to speak. Finally she asked in a very controlled voice, "What?"

"You heard me," Ryder told her, his tone sharp and biting.

Ashley sucked in a breath. "You think I'm going to leave and not tell you where I am?" She could barely get the words out. She swallowed hard and forced the knot in her throat back down.

"You don't have such a great track record, sweetheart. Why in hell should I trust you?" Ryder glared at her, his jaw muscle tight. He felt as if she'd ripped his heart open wide and left it bleeding. She'd known all along that she was pregnant, and she'd never intended to tell him.

"I wouldn't do that."

"You did it before," he reminded her, thinking about how easily the lies had rolled off her seductive lips.

Ashley made herself remain calm. "That was different. You know it was. I'm not going anywhere now. I promise you'll always know where to find me and the baby."

Ryder's hands went to his hips. "Well, darlin', pardon me if I don't quite believe you."

Her breathing hard, Ashley placed a hand on her chest. "I've given you my word," she said, sounding wounded by his distrust. Ryder said nothing. He just stared at her as if her feelings meant absolutely nothing to him.

"All right. I don't care what you think. You'll find out you're wrong. Now, I'm going to raise this child. I planned all along to do it on my own. Just because you know about it doesn't change a thing."

"And how do you plan to do that?" Ryder snapped back, challenging her. "Have you got a big bank account somewhere? Is there a trust fund for you to draw from? Or is your daddy going to help you?"

The dig at her family hit home and her face turned white. "You know I haven't spoken to my father. I don't intend to." Calling upon Jacob Bennett wasn't even a thought. Being on her own meant handling her responsibilities, taking care of herself. The very last person she'd go to for help was her father.

Ryder clenched his teeth. "Well, with the job you have now, darlin', you must barely be able to support yourself. How do you expect to support a baby, also?" he demanded.

"I'm looking for a new job. Bess's daughter is going to take my job at the diner soon, anyway. I'm not stupid, you know. Just because I took the first thing I could find doesn't mean I can't do anything else."

Ryder threw his hands in the air in frustration. "Don't marry me then," he fairly shouted, baring his teeth beneath his mustache. He tried another angle. "I can take care of you and the baby. I'll make sure you're both okay."

"You don't get it, do you?" Ashley asked, waving a hand in front of her like a flag, her lips set firmly in a line.

"Get what?" Ryder asked, irritated that even *that* offer had her glaring at him with fire in her eyes. What was she getting her back up about now?

"I don't want you to take care of me. I don't want you to make sure we're okay. I'm a big girl. I know I can take care of myself, and I can take care of my child. It's what I want to do." Ashley wasn't naive. She knew it wouldn't be easy. But she was convinced she could do it. She'd find the right job, something that would pay her enough to get by on.

Ryder looked at her as if she'd lost her mind. "It's not your child, it's our child. And who's going to raise the baby while you're working? How much is that going to cost? Will you have time for the baby when you get home from work, or will you be too exhausted to spend any time with it?" He fired the questions at her like bullets.

Irritated that he'd voiced the same questions she'd been thinking about for weeks, Ashley snapped, "I haven't worked it all out yet. Besides, I wouldn't be the first mother to leave her child with a sitter while I work." She would feel guilty, but she'd do what she had to do.

Being a single mother was scary, but Ashley could handle it. Despite her own upbringing, she believed the ideal way to raise a child was with a mother and father who loved each other. But she'd learned the hard way, having parents didn't make a child feel loved.

"You're not thinking straight. I can make it easy for you," Ryder told her again, his jaw tight.

"You're being deliberately obtuse."

"And you're driving me crazy!" Ryder stomped from the room and down the stairs.

Ashley went after him, following him into the parlor. He sat on the sofa and pulled on his socks and boots. "What are you doing?"

"Leaving."

Ashley stared at him, her mouth dropping open.

"Oh, I'll be back," Ryder assured her when he caught her expression. He stood and grabbed his hat from the chair where he'd left it the night before. "I just need to get out of here before you make me completely insane."

Ashley tilted her chin. "Fine. Go." *Good riddance,* she added to herself.

"I'm going," Ryder snapped, stomping his way to the front door. He jerked it open, then turned to face her. "This isn't over."

"Yes it is," Ashley replied adamantly.

"We'll see about that." Ryder walked out and slammed the door behind him.

Ashley watched him stalk down the sidewalk and get in his truck. The engine roared to life, and he took off, his tires squealing against the blacktop of the road. She leaned against the door as if she needed it to hold her up.

"Well, that couldn't have gone better," she muttered to herself, then pushed away from the door and went into the parlor. Despite the fact that Ryder had left, there was evidence that he'd been there with her in the most intimate of ways.

Her clothing was strewn on the floor, and the sofa cushions were out of position. Ashley straightened the room, then picked up her clothes. Memories of their lovemaking assailed her, and she sank down on the sofa and wrapped her arms around herself. Tears stung her eyes.

What could one night hurt? Well, now she knew. Damn. If she hadn't gotten sick this morning, Ryder would never have known about the baby. He'd have gone on back to his family and his ranch and would have forgotten all about her.

But would she have forgotten all about him?

Ryder McCall had gotten to her somehow. Jeez, how could she have slept with him again?

But she knew the answer to that. Chemistry. Whatever God had put in a woman and a man to attract them to each other,

PLAY
RUN
FOR THE
ROSES

and get
THREE FREE GIFTS!

HOW TO PLAY:

1. With a coin, carefully scratch off the silver box at the right. Then check the claim chart to see what we have for you — **FREE BOOKS** and a **FREE GIFT** — **ALL YOURS FREE**

2. Send back the card and you'll receive two brand-new Silhouette Desire® novels. These books have a cover price of $3.75 each, but they are yours to keep absolutely free.

3. There's no catch. You're under no obligation to buy anything. We charge nothing — ZERO — for your first shipment. And you don't have to make any minimum number of purchases — not even one!

4. The fact is, thousands of readers enjoy receiving books by mail from the Silhouette Reader Service™. They like the convenience of home delivery...they like getting the best new novels months before they're available in stores...and they love our discount prices

5. We hope that after receiving your free books you'll want to remain a subscriber. But the choice is yours — to continue or cancel, any time at all! So why not take us up on our invitation, with no risk of any kind. You'll be glad you did!

This surprise mystery gift
Will be yours **FREE** –
When you play
RUN for the ROSES

DETACH AND MAIL CARD TODAY!

The Silhouette Reader Service™ — Here's how it works:

Accepting free books places you under no obligation to buy anything. You may keep the books and gift and return the shipping statement marked "cancel." If you do not cancel, about a month later we'll send you 6 additional novels and bill you just $3.12 each, plus 25¢ delivery per book and applicable sales tax, if any.* That's the complete price — and compared to cover prices of $3.75 each — quite a bargain! You may cancel at any time, but if you choose to continue, every month we'll send you 6 more books, which you may either purchase at the discount price...or return to us and cancel your subscription.

*Terms and prices subject to change without notice. Sales tax applicable in N.Y.

If offer card is missing write to: Silhouette Reader Service, 3010 Walden Ave., P.O. Box 1867, Buffalo NY 14240-1867

BUSINESS REPLY MAIL

FIRST-CLASS MAIL   PERMIT NO. 717   BUFFALO, NY

POSTAGE WILL BE PAID BY ADDRESSEE

SILHOUETTE READER SERVICE
3010 WALDEN AVE
PO BOX 1867
BUFFALO NY 14240-9952

NO POSTAGE
NECESSARY
IF MAILED
IN THE
UNITED STATES

He'd given them a huge dose. There was something about Ryder McCall that Ashley just couldn't resist.

"I'm sick and tired of it!"

Ryder heard his sister's declaration before he entered the house. He found Lynn and Jake in the living room, squared off at each other.

"What's going on?" he asked, glancing between them.

"She's in a snit again," Jake answered. Hands on his hips, he glared at their young sister.

"That's it!" Lynn fumed, throwing up her hands in disgust. "If you don't see things my way this time, I'm leaving. I swear I will, Jake." She turned and stalked from the room.

Ryder looked at his brother. "Same old thing?" he asked.

"Yeah. She wants to help Russ with the horses, and he doesn't want her help."

"You have to admit she has a way with horses," Ryder commented.

Jake nodded thoughtfully. "But Russ is the *foreman*. If he doesn't want her help—" He shrugged his big shoulders.

Ryder could see his point, but he could also see Lynn's. She'd been pushing this issue for months, waiting for school to be over. "She's graduated now, and we can't keep her from doing what she wants forever. This is her ranch, too."

"She's barely eighteen. I want her to go to college."

"You can't make her go if she doesn't want to. She seems to know what she wants—" Ryder stopped when he thought about the words he'd said.

I know I can take care of myself and I can take care of my child. It's what I want to do. Ashley's words reverberated through his mind. Funny, he could see what Lynn was trying to say. But when Ashley had said practically the same thing, he hadn't understood.

"I'll be back later," he said to Jake and turned to leave.

"You just got here. Where are you headed now?" Jake asked.

"Back to Rocksprings," Ryder answered and went out the

door. He got in his truck and started the two-hour-plus drive back to Ashley's. Though he was beginning to understand where she was coming from, it didn't mean he trusted her. She'd run out on him once, and she'd lied to him about the baby.

He still wanted Ashley to marry him so his child would be born legitimate, but his first priority was getting her to agree to come to the ranch. Once there, he could keep an eye on her until he could convince her that marriage was the only solution to their problem. Crockett was a small town, and his family was well-known in the area. He'd lived through one humiliating episode when Ariel had dumped him. It looked like he was going to be the butt of even more gossip.

In the meantime, he just needed to come up with an offer that Ashley couldn't pass up.

As he drove down the highway, he thought about the fact that she hadn't intended to tell him about the baby. Though it still rankled him, he'd settled down enough to realize that she'd made that decision based on what little she knew about him.

True, he'd come right out and told her he didn't want to get tied down. And he'd admitted he didn't want kids. But that was before he'd known about the baby—which changed everything. He'd give up his freedom to prevent his child from being labeled a bastard. He didn't understand Ashley. Hell, most women in her condition would have jumped at the chance to marry the father of their child.

Thinking about being a father scared him half to death. He'd never wanted children, and he supposed that came from losing his own parents. Now, because of his own carelessness, he was going to have to face the fact that he was going to be a father. By the time the baby arrived, maybe it wouldn't be such a bad idea.

"Like hell," he muttered, taking the turnoff from the highway. *What a mess, you idiot.* He silently berated himself as he drove to Miss Tilley's. He parked the truck, then went up to the front door and knocked. Ashley had mentioned she had

Sundays off from the diner. He hoped she was still home. A few moments later she slowly opened the door.

Ryder took off his hat and held it in his hands. "I've come in peace," he offered. She didn't say anything, and his gaze searched her face, saw the evidence of her tears. Her eyes were red and swollen. A twinge of regret passed over his expression. "I've cooled off some. The ride gave me time to think about things."

Still, she didn't say anything, didn't make a move to admit him into the house. Ryder couldn't rightly say that he blamed her. He'd been pretty angry before. Sometimes his temper got the best of him. Since they were going to be seeing a lot of each other, he'd either have to rein it in, or she'd learn that he usually simmered down when given some time.

"I know I said some things earlier, most of them in anger," he began. "I'd like another chance to talk this out."

Ashley opened the door wider, but didn't move aside to admit him. "I don't know if I'm up to it. I'm really tired." Actually their lovemaking last night had practically worn her out. This morning her sickness and their argument had zapped what was left of her energy.

"I just want talk. You can throw me out if I get out of line."

Relenting, she let him in and closed the door behind him. He followed her to the parlor. Clearing his throat, he sat on the sofa, then stood again and paced to the other side of the room.

Turning, Ryder looked at Ashley and began to see her in a different light. He couldn't get over the fact that she was carrying his baby. She looked much too young to be a mother. Her hair was in a ponytail, and she wore a baggy pair of pants and a T-shirt that looked two sizes too big. Both effectively hid any indication of her pregnancy.

Apparently her stomach had settled down. There was color to her skin, the pallor once there gone now. She hadn't said anything yet, so he started trying to explain why he was back.

"I drove home and found Lynn and Jake arguing. She

thinks she's old enough to help with the horses, but Jake doesn't. And Russ Logan, our foreman, doesn't want her help.''

Ashley frowned as she listened, growing more confused as he talked. "What does all that have to do with you and me?''

"Well,'' Ryder continued, gesturing with his hands, "I was defending Lynn, trying to make Jake understand that she's old enough to know what she wants.'' He looked into Ashley's eyes. "It made me realize that's what you were trying to make me understand. That you want to decide what's right for you to do.'' He wasn't really lying to her. He understood how she felt—he just didn't agree with her.

Ashley had to give it to him. He'd figured it out after all. "That's right.'' She smiled just a little bit. "It's not that I don't appreciate that you want to help. Despite the fact that you weren't expecting to be a father, I know you want to do the right thing.''

"Maybe it's old-fashioned, but to me, marriage is the honorable solution,'' he said. "I still think it's the best one.''

"Look, I almost got married for the wrong reasons. I won't make the same mistake again.''

Ryder was still quite frustrated. He wanted to insist again that she marry him. Being married to Ashley wouldn't be a hardship. Just thinking about making love to Ashley anytime, anywhere did crazy things to his libido. He shook his head in an effort to dispel his thoughts.

"My mother would skin me alive for getting you pregnant and not marrying you. She taught me her values from a very early age.''

"I understand,'' Ashley said quietly, wishing she'd had the benefit of such a loving parent. "It's just that the right thing for you might not be the right thing for me.''

"What about the right thing for the baby?'' Ryder asked. He wanted her to see it wasn't all cut-and-dried.

"I want what's right for the baby.'' Ashley took a seat on the sofa and looked up at him.

"In most cases, having two parents is the best choice.''

"Not always. Look how I was raised. I don't want my child brought up like that."

Ryder nodded. "But somehow, we've got to agree on what's best for the baby. It might be your body, but it's my child, too. That should count for something." He ran a hand through his hair.

"Of course it does," Ashley assured him. "Maybe I was thinking selfishly when I decided not to tell you, but when you mentioned how you felt about commitments and children, I—" She let the words hang in the air.

Ryder tossed his hat into a nearby chair. "I know I said that, but I'm not totally without feelings. It'll take some getting used to, but I can handle being a father."

"Well, you have about five months to get used to the idea. Now that you know, I have no intention of keeping you from the baby. I just don't want you telling me what I can or can't do."

"Yeah, right." He looked at her, his gaze intense. "We haven't had much of a chance to get to know each other," he told her, thinking they'd spent much of their time in bed making love. "I can be pretty stubborn sometimes."

Ashley looked at him, a small smile lighting her eyes. "No, you're kidding." Ryder grinned, and she felt the sparkle of his blue gaze as it passed over her.

"Yeah, well, I can be full of charm, too, darlin'," he told her smugly.

Ashley could believe it. He'd *charmed* her several times. That's how she'd gotten into this mess. "What do we do now?" she asked, wondering where this was leading.

"Well, since you won't marry me, I think I have a solution that we can agree on. Just keep an open mind and take a few days to think it over. I'll leave and go back home and you can call me when you've made up your mind."

Eight

"Okay, I give," Ashley said, her curiosity piqued. Marriage would have been the most logical solution if they were in love. Though she did feel something for him, she hadn't put a tag on those feelings and she didn't intend to. She wasn't willing to let her heart get any more deeply involved.

"You promise to at least think about what I have to say?" Ryder asked, wanting to be sure that she wouldn't fly off the handle when she heard his idea.

"I promise."

"How about if I offer you a job?" Ryder had thought of this solution on his way there. Having her live at the ranch was the only way he'd be sure she wouldn't take off again. And maybe, after he got her there, she'd think about marrying him, especially if he worked on her a bit. He watched her expression to gauge her reaction. She frowned a little, then the idea seemed to sink in.

"A job?" Ashley asked, and immediately wondered what he was up to. "Doing what?"

Ryder shrugged. He had several ideas floating around in his head. "I don't know. I'm sure there's something you could do at the ranch."

Ashley shook her head adamantly. "I don't see where that's any different from wanting to take care of me. I don't want you to invent a job for me."

"I'm not," Ryder insisted. "We're always needing help with something. You could cook or clean. Better yet, how are you at figures, accounting, that kind of thing?"

"Pretty good, I guess," she answered, unsure of where this was going. "I don't know accounting, but I took bookkeeping in school. I liked it a lot."

"There you go. Right now Lynn takes care of the accounts. She could teach you how to do them."

Ashley shook her head. "I don't want to interfere with your sister's work. How would she like that?"

"Actually, it could be a perfect solution. She wants to work with the horses, and Jake's held her back as long as he can. I don't see that he's going to have any choice but to give in to her, whether our foreman likes it or not."

"And hiring me to do the accounts would free her to do that," Ashley concluded.

Ryder took a seat at the far end of the sofa, sitting on the edge. "Exactly."

Ashley replied, "Look, I don't want to get in the middle of a family quarrel." She'd had enough of living unhappily to last her a lifetime.

"It won't be like that. Jake will see that he doesn't really have much choice but to let Lynn give it a try. She's threatening to leave the ranch, and he'll do anything to keep her there."

"I don't know," Ashley said, her forehead creasing as she thought about it. Working at the McCall ranch wasn't something she would have considered in her wildest dreams.

Ryder braced a hand against his knee. He felt if she agreed, he'd at least be able to be sure that she and the baby were all right. If she lived at the ranch, he could keep track of her, even if she didn't marry him, which he didn't plan on settling for. She and the baby were his responsibility, whether she thought so or not. "Just think about it. This is a great solution. You'd earn a good salary and have a roof over your head."

After hearing the last part of his offer, Ashley realized that no matter what she'd said, he still didn't trust her. "Forget it. I'm not living at your ranch." There was no way she was going to live that close to him. Her heart had been racing since he'd returned. Just being in the room with him was enough to make her remember what it was like to make love with him.

"Why the hell not?" Ryder barked, immediately offended.

"I've already explained it to you. I'm not going over it again." Ashley was becoming agitated. First he understood, then he didn't. She wished he would make up his mind.

Ryder slapped his thigh, then suggested, "Look, just give it a chance. If it doesn't work out, if you find it uncomfortable, you can find a place in town to rent." He really didn't like that idea, but getting her on the ranch was his first objective. He'd worry about keeping her there later. "This is the best solution for both of us and the baby."

He didn't blame her for not trusting him. She had good reason not to trust men. But they were even on that score because he didn't trust her, either. "Think about it. I'm not offering you a free ride. You'll be working for what you make. Keeping the books isn't an easy job. Lynn's computerized everything, but we have a big operation."

"I know a little bit about computers," Ashley admitted cautiously. "We had several at our house."

"There you go," Ryder said and his face relaxed a little. He forged ahead with his best ammunition. "Another thing to think about is how much this child will be loved by my family. You know what it was like being raised without love, without affection. I know you don't want that for our child. My family will welcome you and the baby with open arms. It'll grow up with more attention than you can even fathom. And we'll all be there to help you take care of it.

"While you're working, the baby can be right with you,"

he reasoned. "You'll be the one taking care of it instead of some sitter. You'll hear the baby's first word, watch it take its first steps. How many jobs could you get that you'd have that option?"

Ashley knew that answer. Next to none. "How is your family going to feel about all this?" she asked.

"Lynn will be happy to have someone near her own age to talk to."

"What about your brothers? How are they going to feel when you tell them about me?" Ashley couldn't believe she was actually giving the idea consideration.

"I'll talk to them tonight. I really don't expect any problem, though. We all take part in running the ranch, and sometimes that means making decisions when the others aren't around to consult."

"I need to think about this, Ryder. It sounds like a great offer," she rushed on when his expression began to change. She was beginning to learn all about his stubborn streak. "I just can't make a decision this important too quickly."

Ryder stood at that point and nodded. "That's all I ask. Give it some thought. I really feel like this is the right thing to do." He hesitated, then added, "If you're not happy, you don't have to stay. We'll work out something else."

"Would you mind if I called you in a couple of days? That would give you time to talk to your family." And give her time to think about it fully. Ashley knew she didn't always think straight when she was around Ryder McCall.

"All right," Ryder agreed, though he sounded disappointed that she hadn't jumped at his offer. He reached into his back pocket and took out his wallet. Extracting a business card, he handed it to her. "That's my number. Call me anytime."

Ashley flashed him a quick smile. "Thanks."

For a moment they were both silent.

"Uh, I guess that's all I had to say," Ryder said, grabbing his hat and making his way to the door. Ashley followed and stopped when he turned around. "I'm sorry if I upset you earlier. I didn't mean to."

Ashley thought his apology came reluctantly, but she accepted it, anyway. "You had every right to be angry. I should have told you about the baby."

"Are you feeling all right now?" he asked, wondering about her. She looked better. As a matter of fact, she looked downright gorgeous. His loins tightened, which seemed to be an automatic reaction whenever he was near her. It was going to be hard to be around her and not touch her.

"Yes. It passes pretty quickly once I get some food down."

"That's good." He was hesitant to leave, but didn't think it was a good idea to overstay his welcome. She seemed willing to think over his offer so he'd gotten over that hurdle. "Well, I guess I'll talk to you soon."

Ashley nodded her head. "I'll call you."

With nothing more to keep him there, Ryder turned and walked out the door.

Once again Ashley watched him go, but this time there was a slight lift in her heartbeat.

Ryder McCall had truly surprised her. He might not have wanted any ties, but he'd sure accepted responsibility for his child without being forced to. She had to admire him for that.

Ashley spent the rest of the day tidying Miss Tilley's house for her return. During that time, she gave a lot of thought to Ryder's offer. She knew it was to her benefit to take him up on it. With Bess's daughter getting out of school in two weeks, she'd be out of a job. If she worked at Ryder's ranch, she'd have plenty of time to find something else if she wanted.

She felt sure that she could learn to keep the ranch accounts. And to be able to take care of her baby while working, well, that was an advantage that weighed heavily in favor of accepting.

She sensed that Ryder still didn't trust her, and she supposed she deserved that. She hadn't been honest with him. Given time, he'd find out that she would never deny him his child.

Ryder's arguments had reminded her of one thing. There was no chance that her baby would ever know her family. If she lived at the ranch, the baby would grow up around people who would love it. Could she deny her own flesh and blood the kind of love and affection that she had hungered for?

There were so many advantages to accepting Ryder's offer. And one main problem. She'd have to see Ryder, probably a lot. She didn't think she'd have to worry about his feelings. She thought as her pregnancy progressed, any attraction he felt for her would subside.

But Ashley knew she'd have to deal with her feelings for him. She thought that she already had, until he came back into her life. She sighed as she carried her things to her room. There was no future where Ryder McCall was concerned. He wasn't looking for love. And she didn't believe in it anymore, anyway.

Ashley spent two days deliberating over her decision. First she would decide to accept, then she would decide not to. Ryder called her the evening of the second day.

"How are you feeling?" he asked right away.

"Better," she answered, touched by the concern in his voice. She was glad to hear from him. Though she had told him she would call, the fact that he'd called made her feel that he'd been thinking about her, too. Well, at least he'd been thinking about the baby.

"That's good." There was a long, awkward pause. "I, uh, wanted you to know that I've discussed the situation with my brothers and sister. They've completely agreed with my suggestion that you come to work for us."

"Are you sure?" Ashley asked hesitantly. Despite his assurances, she still felt as if she was being thrust upon them.

"Yeah. I wanted you to know, just in case it had anything to do with your decision."

Well, of course it did, Ashley thought, relieved to hear that Ryder's family had given him their support. That said a lot about them. Obviously they were the kind of family who pulled together in a crisis. Unlike hers.

"That's really nice of them." She paused, then asked, "Would you mind if I took one more day to think it over?" Silence filled the line.

"No, not at all," he told her.

Though she could tell from his tone he wasn't pleased about waiting, Ashley thanked him, then hung up the telephone. She thought he sounded a little disappointed when she'd told him that she hadn't made up her mind. She couldn't say why, but that made her feel good inside.

The next morning when she awoke, Ashley stretched and yawned, opening her eyes slowly. She rested her hand on her belly and immediately felt her stomach jump. Her heart raced, excitement spreading through her. Her baby moved! It was such a profound moment, Ashley nearly cried.

She was nurturing a life: a baby she'd love and cherish, who would love her as much. She had a chance to start over now, to raise her child with the kind of affection and caring she'd never had.

It was then that she made her decision. She wanted what was best for her child, and that included being close to its father. She would take Ryder up on his offer. It would provide a way for her to care for her baby, and if it didn't work out, she'd follow through with her first plan.

She called Ryder later that morning with her decision. Ashley explained that she wanted to finish out her job with Bess. He seemed to understand, and they set a date for her to move.

Ten days later Ryder and Deke parked at Miss Tilley's.

"This where she's been living?" Deke asked. He'd come with Ryder to drive Ashley's car back to the ranch. They hadn't talked much. Ryder had been in a mood, and Deke had known better than to push him.

"Yeah." Ryder stared at the house, mixed feelings running through him. He hadn't seen Ashley in almost two weeks, had only talked to her a couple of times. Anticipation made his heart race. "Let's go."

The two men got out of Ryder's truck and walked to the door. Miss Tilley answered and let them inside.

"Ashley's upstairs," she said, her eyes watchful. "She'll be down in a minute."

Ryder looked around the foyer. He saw several bags packed and recognized a couple of them as Ashley's. His nerves calmed somewhat. The bags meant she hadn't changed her mind. Until now he'd known that was a possibility. His plan was working. "You boys can wait in the parlor while I get Ashley," Miss Tilley said.

Moments later Ashley entered the room and Ryder's gaze locked with hers. Ryder had always thought she was beautiful. Today, though, she seemed to glow.

He'd heard somewhere that pregnant women did that, but had never seen it firsthand. He felt an unexpected surge of possessiveness that he had to clamp down. A muscle in his jaw flexed as he looked away.

"This is Deke," Ryder said, sounding a lot more at ease than he felt. "Deke, you remember Ashley. And this is Miss Tilley."

Deke McCall stuck out his hand. "Ashley. You're as pretty as I remember." He winked at her, his eyes twinkling. "Ma'am," he said, and shook Miss Tilley's hand before turning his full attention back to Ashley.

Ashley forced her gaze from Ryder to his younger brother and found it hard to believe that there were two McCalls so alike, yet so different. Also blond-haired and blue-eyed, Deke had a lazy smile and a laid-back manner that helped to put her at ease.

"Thank you." She smiled at him and was pleased when he gave her a boyish grin. "And thanks for coming with Ryder." Ashley had agreed when Ryder had suggested bringing Deke to drive her car to the ranch. She was still having the morning sickness and she tired easily.

"No problem. Glad to be of help."

Ashley looked again at Ryder. His expression was so intense that her smile slipped a little. She wondered what he was thinking. "I'm ready now if you are." She handed Deke her keys.

Deke and Ryder carried her cases out while she said goodbye to Miss Tilley. He was waiting by the truck when she came down the walkway.

"Everything all right?" he asked, a frown creasing his forehead when he noticed her tears.

Ashley nodded. "Yes. I'm just being silly, I guess. I'd kind of gotten used to living here. I didn't think it would be so hard to leave."

"That's understandable." Ryder figured she'd found peace here. And friends. Those things were hard to replace. He hoped she'd find the same things in Crockett.

She sniffed and wiped at her eyes, feeling a little embarrassed to be crying. "Saying goodbye to Bess was hard."

"You can come back anytime to see her," he suggested, trying to say something that would make her feel better. He opened the door to the cab, then gave her a hand getting inside his truck.

Once she was seated, Ryder quickly released her, then shut the door and walked around the truck, his mind turning with thoughts that had nothing to do with the drive and everything to do with his attraction to Ashley. How the hell was he going to handle it?

He climbed in behind the wheel, feeling as if he was being put to a test. He was still angry with her for not telling him about the baby. And he couldn't say he trusted her. But he was also plenty attracted to her. He felt like he was at war with himself. Before he started the engine, he looked at her. "Are you sure you have everything?"

Ashley nodded. "I haven't bought much since I've been here. Just a few clothes and some necessities," she explained. She looked behind them as he started the truck and pulled away from Miss Tilley's, noticing that Deke was already gone.

Ryder followed her gaze with his own, then turned back to watch where he was driving. "Deke'll meet us at the ranch. He has your bags with him."

As they rode through the town, Ryder saw the sheriff standing on a corner talking with someone. He looked up when the truck passed, and Ashley raised her hand to wave at him. She sniffed again and Ryder's jaw clenched. He wondered if Ashley had said goodbye to the sheriff, as well.

Hell, it didn't matter. She was with him now, he told himself. Still, the knot in his gut twisted a little more.

Ashley couldn't seem to relax. Now that the time to move had arrived, she was beginning to feel nervous. How did Ryder's family really feel about her coming to the ranch to live? She clenched her hands in her lap and looked out at the passing fields. She'd made the right decision, she reminded herself. Everything would work out.

They fell into silence as he headed north on Highway 277, neither of them seeming to have much to say. Ryder stopped in Sonora for her to use the bathroom. She needed to do that more often now. He got her a cold can of cola and one for himself. They were back on the road before too long.

"We're only about forty-five minutes away," he told her as he drove west on Interstate 10. Ashley smiled at him, yet it seemed forced. He'd noticed the way her hand rested protectively on her stomach. It made him wonder if she was feeling all right.

His thoughts had him all wound up. Knowing she was carrying his baby did strange things to his insides. He had expected the fact that she was pregnant to turn him off. Instead, he was finding it harder than ever not to touch her.

Ryder was quiet for a few minutes, trying to get up enough nerve to broach a subject he didn't really want to discuss. The closer he got to the ranch, the more he seemed to tense.

"I was wondering," he finally said, gathering his courage. "Uh, have you been to a doctor, yet? You know, about the baby." He glanced quickly in her direction, then away. Heat surged to his face, and he cursed silently. This wasn't something he felt comfortable discussing. Cows he knew something about. Babies were a different story. He'd never had much contact with a pregnant woman.

Ashley turned in her seat just enough to be able to see him. She didn't miss the tint of red beneath his tanned skin. "I saw a doctor a few times. He put me on special vitamins." Ashley thought it was kind of cute the way he avoided looking at her and kept his eyes straight ahead on the road.

Ryder swallowed hard. "Is everything, uh, you know, okay?" This had to be the hardest conversation he'd ever had.

"Yes, I think so." Ashley told him. "I'll have to find a new doctor, though."

Ryder cut his gaze to her, then just as quickly he looked away. "The nearest decent-sized town to the ranch is San Luis. It's not a metropolis, but it has a pretty up-to-date hospital. We have to pass through it to get to the ranch, which is just on the other side of Ozona."

She looked at him speculatively and he explained, "I busted a couple of ribs a while back. I don't know about having babies, but they took good care of me." He glanced at her belly, and his face reddened even more as heat spread down his neck. "Are you nervous about it?"

"I'd be lying if I said no," she admitted.

Ryder sat up straighter, adjusting himself in his seat, trying to get his mind off how good she looked and smelled—the effect she had on him. "I don't know how much help I'll be, but I'm willing to try and go through this with you." Being the baby's father, Ryder felt it was his duty. He couldn't help it if he didn't feel too enthusiastic about it.

Ashley could tell Ryder wasn't exactly comfortable with the idea. "It's kind of you to offer," she said noncommittally.

He shot another glance at her stomach. "You wouldn't be in that condition if I'd been responsible enough to protect you."

Ashley shook her head. "It took both of us to make this baby."

"Yeah, I know." Ryder knew that for sure. He hadn't forgotten a thing about what it was like to make love to her. And he knew he wanted to again.

"You don't need to blame yourself, Ryder," Ashley told him, turning back to face the road. "You don't owe me anything and I'm not expecting anything from you."

Ryder wondered how she could be so blasé about it. Maybe

it was because she'd been forced to do things she'd never wanted to do. Maybe it was because she'd never been able to rely on someone to stand up for her. Well, that didn't matter. She was his responsibility, whether she wanted to be or not. He'd learned one thing for sure: she wanted to be independent, and he'd have to be sure she felt that way. But that didn't mean he'd give up on getting her to marry him.

"I don't want to argue with you over this," he told her, keeping his tone even. "I just want to be sure you're okay, and the best way to do that is to be involved."

Ashley became silent. Once again he'd made it clear that he felt responsible for her because she was carrying his child. She didn't need to be hit with a brick. Anything else he felt came from below his waist. She'd do well to remember it.

Ryder didn't say much from that point on, so Ashley didn't force conversation. They passed through Ozona, then the small town of Crockett, which consisted of little more than a drugstore, a general store and a bank. They had traveled about ten minutes longer when he finally spoke.

"I thought I'd better warn you. My family can be kind of overwhelming at times. Lynn's pretty excited about you coming. She's already made up one of the spare bedrooms." Ashley flashed her eyes in his direction.

"I hope she didn't go to too much trouble. I still feel a little awkward about being at the ranch. I could get a room at a motel for a while, since I don't really know if staying at the ranch is going to work out."

Ryder shook his head and grinned. "Well, yeah, darlin', you could at that. But you're going to have to be the one who tells Lynn."

Ryder looked at Ashley and noticed that she'd clenched her hands in her lap. "Anxious?" he asked.

Ashley's response was a shaky smile. "Wouldn't you be?"

"I reckon so. But I think you'll like my family, once you get to know them. Lynn can be a handful, but she's got a big heart and she's kind and loyal. Deke, well, you've met him. He's pretty much like you've seen. Easygoing and full of himself. Jake's a little harder to get to know. He doesn't say too much, so don't think he doesn't want you there.''

"I'll try to remember that," Ashley replied.

Ryder nodded. "We're here."

Nine

Ryder turned down a blacktopped road. It wound up a hillside, trees lining both sides of it. When they cleared, there was a large wood-and-iron sign welcoming visitors to the Bar M Ranch.

As the truck came over a small ridge, Ashley saw fenced pastures and several large outbuildings. There was also a narrow airstrip with a Cessna parked outside a hangar. It quickly became apparent that Ryder hadn't truly impressed upon her how large their operation really was. This wasn't a just family-run business; it was a small dynasty.

Ashley watched as they passed fenced pastures, a gigantic barn and what looked like a long row of stalls. When she caught a glimpse of the main house, her breath caught. She'd had no idea that his family's ranch was so immense or that he lived in such a beautiful home. The large ranch-style structure was extremely well kept. It sat nestled in a small grove of trees, a neat flower garden adorning it.

"Oh, my, it's beautiful here. And what a lovely home."

"Thanks. My dad built it when I was fifteen. My parents only lived in it for a few months before they were killed." He pulled to a stop in front of the house.

Ryder hadn't told her how his parents had died, and it seemed apparent from his tone that he wasn't used to talking about them. She wondered if he was always so quiet about things that bothered him.

"It's magnificent," she said, taking in her surroundings.

"Do you keep horses or cattle?" she asked.

"Both." Ryder opened his door, then came around for her. "We started out with cattle, then got into horses as a side business. We train quarter horses."

"I'm impressed," she said with all honesty. Ryder gave her a fleeting smile, which momentarily turned his mustache up at the corners.

"We do our best."

Before Ashley could say anything else, a young woman came out of the front door and hurried down the steps. She was definitely a McCall. She had most of the markings, blond hair, gorgeous blue eyes and a friendly smile. She wasn't striking, but she was pretty and petite. Ashley was warmed by the way her eyes lit with enthusiasm.

"Hi! You've got to be Ashley. Ryder's told us about you, but not nearly enough." She shot her brother an affectionate look.

Ryder put his arm around his sister. "This is Lynn, the brat of the family." Lynn socked him in the arm and he winced. "Behave." He playfully smacked her on her fanny. "This is Ashley Bennett."

"I'm so happy to meet you," Lynn said, grinning while she rubbed her backside.

"Thank you for having me. I hope you didn't go to any trouble on my account," Ashley said. It was obvious the two had a lot of love between them. Though she thought it was wonderful, in a strange way she felt saddened, also. She was reminded again of how much she'd missed by not growing up with a loving family.

Lynn linked her arm with Ashley's and ushered her toward the door, talking as if she'd known Ashley all her life. Ashley was quite startled by Lynn's warm welcome and caught only her last sentence before she stopped talking.

"I've been so excited about meeting you."

Ashley glanced back at Ryder, who was walking close behind them. She wasn't used to someone so warmhearted and cordial. "It's a pleasure to meet you, too." And it was. She envied Lynn's passionate personality. Growing up, Ashley had never been allowed to express herself so freely. She had a feeling they could easily be friends.

Lynn showed her around the house. It was a sprawling structure with six bedrooms. Exposed beams supported the ceiling in the den, which also had a stone fireplace. The kitchen was rather large and had all the modern appliances. Ryder trailed behind them, his boots pounding against the immaculate wood floors.

Chatting away, Lynn led the way to the bedroom she'd prepared. Ashley felt Ryder's hand on her back as they stepped into the room. Shivers ran up her spine, reminding her of all the things he made her feel, how much she wanted him...and that she could easily lose her heart to him.

"Deke already put your bags in here. He arrived a little while ago," Lynn informed her. She turned and gave Ashley a hug. "I'm so glad you're here." She smiled and looked genuinely happy.

"Thank you," Ashley replied, a little taken aback by Lynn's impulsive show of emotion. She had grown up without any display of affection. This was going to take some getting used to.

"Take your time unpacking. When you're done, I'll show you around the ranch."

"She might be tired, Lynn," Ryder interjected, reading Ashley's bewildered expression. "Give her a chance to breathe."

"Oh, I'm sorry," Lynn apologized quickly, then touched Ashley's shoulder with her hand. "Of course you are. Please let me know if you need anything. All of us want you to feel at home here. I'll leave you in my brother's good hands.'' Her eyes sparkled as she gave him a wink. ''We can visit more later.''

Ashley assured her she would, and Lynn left. Once again Ashley was alone in a bedroom with Ryder McCall. She took a deep breath as she turned to face him, feeling as if she'd been caught in a whirlwind and was just coming down from it. For such a small, delicate person, Lynn McCall was like a little ball of fire. ''Well, your sister is certainly...'' She hesitated, searching for the right word.

''Overwhelming,'' Ryder finished for her. ''I tried to warn you.'' His gaze slid away from hers. He hoped she didn't take offense at Lynn's manner. He'd never known anyone his sister couldn't get along with, except maybe their foreman. ''She takes some getting used to.''

Ashley smiled at him as his gaze came back to her. ''She's very nice. And very pretty. You all look quite a lot alike.''

''You haven't met Jake, yet,'' Ryder said, thinking of his older brother. ''His eyes are brown and his hair is dark brown. All of us joke about him being left on the doorstep and adopted.'' He grinned at her. ''Actually, he's the only one who takes after my father's side of the family. The rest of us look like our mother.''

Ashley nodded as she walked around the room to familiarize herself. ''Is this a picture of your parents?'' she asked, noticing a framed photograph on the dresser.

''Yeah. It's the last picture they had taken together before they were killed in a plane crash.''

Ashley moved closer to him to see the photo. His parents looked so happy. And much too young to have died. ''I'm sorry. I know it must have been hard on all of you,'' she said, her voice nearly a whisper. She had a feeling that it had been especially hard for him. It seemed to her that even though many years had passed, he still felt a tremendous amount of sorrow.

"Mostly for Jake," Ryder told her. "He quit college to raise us and keep the ranch going."

"I'm sure your parents would have been very proud of all of you."

Ryder looked away. "Yeah." Without saying anything more, he shifted his stance, then tucked his hands in the front pockets of his jeans. "I thought maybe you'd want to rest for a while," he suggested, changing the subject.

Ashley touched her stomach, as the baby chose that moment to stir. She wore a thin pair of cotton slacks and could feel her belly move slightly. Her surprise registered on her face and her eyes flew up to meet Ryder's.

"What is it?" he asked. His gaze fell to where her hand rested. Immediately he was alarmed. "Maybe you should sit down," he suggested, unsure of what to do.

Before she had a chance to answer, he was beside her and guiding her to the bed. "I'm fine, really," Ashley insisted, amused by his reaction.

Ryder sat on the bed beside her, his weight shifting her closer to him. He slipped his arm around her shoulders. "Are you sure?" The look on her face had about scared him half to death.

Ashley turned to look at him, her heart pounding from all the emotions bouncing around inside her. If experiencing the baby's movement wasn't enough, his nearness was sending shock waves straight to her heart. When she looked into his blue eyes, her breath caught.

"What was it? Is the baby okay?"

Ashley shook her head, her gaze never leaving his. "The baby moved. I'm not quite used to it yet." She marveled at how it made her feel. It was scary, yet exciting.

"You can feel the baby moving already?" Ryder asked and sounded amazed.

"Not all the time. So when he does, he surprises me." Her voice dropped to a whisper. "Would you like to feel it?" she asked.

"I guess." Ryder was still a little anxious about all this

baby stuff. Until now, the baby seemed unreal, though he
knew that was just his way of dealing with it.

Ashley took his hand and gently pressed it to her stomach.
"He doesn't move very often yet," she told him again, not
wanting him to be disappointed.

"He?" Ryder repeated, his mind more on Ashley than the
baby they'd created. He moved closer, close enough to breathe
in the essence of her. His response to touching her was immediate. Blood thickened in his veins, making his heart pound
even harder. He wanted, needed to take her mouth with his.

Ashley's gaze dropped to his lips, which were mere inches
from hers. "Um, I don't really know. That's just how I refer
to the baby."

The baby hadn't moved again, yet Ryder kept his hand on
her belly, not wanting to end the intimacy between them. He
knew it was crazy, but he just had to taste her again—just for
a moment.

He whispered her name, then bent to touch his mouth to
hers, expecting her to resist. Her eyelids lowered, and she
didn't pull away, didn't move an inch. Ryder traced her lips
with his tongue. "Open your mouth for me," he whispered,
his voice low and thick.

Ashley complied as he slipped his tongue past her teeth to
taste her fully. She moved closer to him, and he deepened the
kiss, completely covering her mouth with his. His blood
warmed. He wondered how he ever thought he'd be able to
live without touching her, kissing her, making love to her. He
lifted his mouth and began to trace kisses down her throat,
knowing he should pull away, but unable to make himself do
so.

He started to take her mouth again when he felt her stomach
move. Instantly Ryder pulled away and stood, distancing himself from her as he silently cursed himself. He'd forgotten
about the baby. All he'd been thinking about was wanting
Ashley, being inside her. This was crazy! He felt as if he was
on a roller-coaster ride and wasn't able to get off.

Ashley froze, stunned by his reaction. "I'm sorry. I thought you'd want to experience the baby moving." She'd learned her lesson. She wouldn't press him again.

"It isn't that," Ryder said, unable to express what he was feeling. "Well, not exactly."

Ashley wanted to ask what *exactly* it was, but caught herself. It was obvious that he wasn't really ready to accept the baby into his heart or his life. He'd said he wanted to help her through the pregnancy. Now she knew that his offer had just been lip service. From this point on, she wouldn't count on him at all.

"I'm really tired. If you don't mind, I think I'll rest awhile." She didn't even look at him.

Ryder moved toward the door, aware that he'd hurt her. He couldn't find the words at that moment to explain his behavior. Hell, he wasn't even sure what he was feeling anymore. "I'll check on you later."

"That isn't necessary. I'll come down in a little bit."

Ryder left the room, his expression grim.

Well, hell! It seemed that when it came to Ashley, he couldn't do or say anything right. He hadn't meant to react that way when the baby moved. It had just surprised him, that's all. He'd been thinking of making love to her, and the baby moving had been like a bucket of cold water dumped over him.

Ryder stormed through the house, passing through the back porch and out the back door, slamming it behind him. He didn't stop until he was at the barn. He saddled his horse, mounted and took off, deciding to spend a few hours riding range. He wasn't fit company and he needed some time to think.

Hours later he rode back in, feeling as if he'd wasted his time. Though he'd checked the fences around the south pasture and noted a couple of places that needed repair, he hadn't come to terms with what he was going to do about his feelings for Ashley.

It was strange. The days he hadn't seen her had slowly driven him crazy. He'd tried to stay busy and keep his mind on his work, but she'd always been in his thoughts. Ryder had told himself that once she was at the ranch, he'd be able to keep his distance from her, give her the space she seemed to need.

Fat chance.

He wasn't sure what kind of relationship they would have, but being friends just wasn't going to cut it. He still wanted her to marry him, so his baby would have his name. Though now, with Ashley hurt and upset, it wasn't a good time to bring up the idea again. He thought about the kiss they'd shared earlier. She hadn't rejected him, which told him she had some feelings for him. It didn't matter to him that whatever was between them was just physical.

He knew it wasn't love, and he had no intention of falling in love with her. His experience with Ariel had left his heart bitter. God, he'd been a fool. Her piercing laughter still struck a tender cord when he let himself remember his humiliation. Well, he wasn't going to put himself through that kind of hell again by becoming emotionally involved with Ashley. But that didn't mean that he didn't want her. He'd been aching for her all afternoon.

No matter what happened, he had to deal with the fact that he was going to be a father. He could do that. He'd make sure his child never needed anything.

He cooled his horse down, then headed for the house to check on Ashley. He wanted to explain why he'd reacted the way he had earlier, though he wasn't sure he'd be able to put it into words.

Ashley glanced toward the door when she heard it open. She quickly looked away when Ryder entered.

"Well, hey, Ryder," Lynn greeted him with her usual bright smile. "Ashley and I were just getting acquainted."

"That's good. Have you met Jake, yet?" He directed his question to Ashley to force her to look at him. She was standing next to Lynn, a dish towel in her hands. She turned to face him, her gaze landing somewhere behind him.

"Not yet." Her answer was clipped and to the point.

"You'll meet him at dinner, more than likely. How are you feeling?" he asked, watching her closely.

"I'm fine," she answered shortly.

"Dinner won't be for a while," Lynn said, breaking into the conversation. "I hope you got something to eat while you were out. Or I can make you a sandwich if you want one."

"I'm not hungry," Ryder answered, shaking his head.

Lynn gave him a curious look. "You must be sick. I've never known you to turn down food."

"Well, I'm not sick," he replied stiffly, "I'm just not hungry." He shifted his stance. He wanted to talk to Ashley, but not in front of his sister. "Would you like to see a little of the ranch?" he asked Ashley, once again forcing her to look at him.

"I'm helping Lynn with dinner preparations," she said, and seemed glad to have an excuse to refuse.

Lynn took the towel from her. "Oh, go ahead. I can do the rest by myself." She gave Ashley a little shove. "There's not much left to do."

Ashley looked from Lynn to Ryder. "All right," she agreed. He stood aside and motioned for her to precede him out the door.

Once outside, Ashley noticed how late it was getting. He'd been gone a long time, and she'd wondered what he'd been doing, though she wasn't about to ask Lynn where he might be. They walked in silence for a few minutes. Ryder started talking about the ranch as he showed her around, pretty much avoiding looking directly at her.

He introduced her to Russ Logan, who was a handsome man, with brown hair and a slim build and strong arms. But Ashley noticed an emptiness in his green eyes that made her wonder about him.

The barn was a huge red-painted structure with a fenced corral on the side of it. They stepped inside and Ashley was immediately cognizant of the potent smell of hay and horses. As she listened, she found there was a lot she didn't know about ranching.

Ryder seemed careful to keep his distance, as if he wasn't sure he should touch her, or didn't want to. She wasn't sure which. She guessed it didn't matter. He'd made his feelings known when he'd bolted from her and avoided her for hours.

He showed her some of the horses, stopping at the last stall to introduce his own horse, Blaze, a large black animal that Ashley found a bit threatening. She listened as he talked, looking at the animal instead of at him.

Finally he focused his gaze on Ashley and said, "I'm sorry about what happened earlier."

Ashley turned to look at him then, her eyes distant and cool. "It's okay," she whispered, the hurt still inside her. It was better this way, she told herself. She turned to leave, stopping only when he reached out and gently grasped her arm.

"I'd like to try and explain," Ryder said, his gaze searching hers.

"It isn't necessary," she replied quickly, feeling the effect of his touch run through her. She shrugged free of his hand and he let her go.

Ashley looked at him then. He seemed as uncomfortable as she felt. "Look, maybe this was a bad idea."

"What?" he asked, not following her.

"My coming here. Maybe I should just find a job in San Luis. I've got some money saved, enough to get by on for a while." She lifted her chin just a little to show him she meant it.

Ryder shook his head. "That's already been settled. You promised to take over for Lynn. She's counting on you."

"I'm sure you can find someone else."

Ryder swore and stepped back, away from her. "I don't want to find someone else."

Ashley stared back at him, thinking for a moment that he'd meant more than his words implied. She finally said, "Well you could have fooled me. It's obvious you're uncomfortable about this baby," she told him, remembering how he'd pulled away when the baby moved. It made her heart twist with pain. Her father hadn't cared about her, either. She wasn't going to let her child grow up like she did, with a father that didn't really love it.

"I wanted to explain about that." His expression was contrite, as if he regretted the incident. "I guess even though I knew you were pregnant, somehow it just wasn't real to me. Then, when the baby moved, it all sort of came into focus. Just give me some time, Ashley. I haven't known about the baby that long. I know it doesn't seem like it, but I really do care about it."

"I'd like to believe you, but I can't." She eyed him cautiously. "Either you want to be a part of the baby's life or you don't. Which is it?" she asked pointedly.

"I do." Ryder's mouth tightened. "All I'm asking for is a little time."

Ashley stilled, then straightened her back. "How much time?" she asked, her throat tight with emotion. He didn't say anything, just looked at her in silence.

Ashley turned and walked away from him. She left the barn and started for the house, her heart heavy. Ryder kept insisting that he wanted to be a part of the baby's life, but his actions, his response to the baby, said otherwise. Maybe a little time was what he needed. She hoped so. Because her child was not going to grow up like her, unwanted and unloved.

When Ashley arrived in the kitchen, Lynn was about finished with dinner preparations. Ashley helped carry the food to the dining room table, which Lynn had already set.

Deke came in first, and Ashley was relieved he wasn't Ryder. He talked with her a few minutes and had a way of making her feel at home. She laughed when he recounted a few stories about ranch life, enjoying his sense of humor. Ryder picked that moment to enter the kitchen, his boots thudding heavily as he walked over to them, a frown on his handsome face. Ashley's expression suddenly sobered.

"Hey, bro'," Deke said, still chuckling and unaware of the undercurrents between his brother and Ashley. "I was just telling Ashley about that time Dad caught you playing with matches and made you paint the barn."

Ryder grinned as expected, but the humor of the situation never made it to his eyes. He should have been pleased that Ashley was getting along with his family, but it bothered him to see her acting so friendly with Deke. "Is dinner ready?" He directed his question to Lynn.

"Yes. We're just waiting on Jake." Lynn went into the dining room, carrying a tray of biscuits.

"I'm here," Jake called, stepping into the room from the back porch.

"Jake, this is Ashley Bennett," Ryder said, introducing Ashley to his brother.

Ashley's gaze flickered from Ryder to Jake, who nodded at her. He gave her a brief smile, and her anxiety eased. She had expected some resentment from him, considering he wasn't happy about letting Lynn work with the foreman and the horses. Ashley felt her presence had sort of forced the issue.

"Welcome to the family, Ashley."

Though his voice was gruff, Jake sounded as if he meant it. His dark eyes studied her with shrewd intensity. Their gazes locked and Ashley saw a hardness in his eyes that made him seem a lot older than he was.

"Thank you," she answered, some of the tension easing out of her. She felt dwarfed by the three men. All of them were tall, and hard muscled. Jake, however, had a rigid edge to his handsome features. Deke was leaner and his face still held the boyish handsomeness of youth. Her gaze slid to Ryder. She wondered if she and Ryder were the only ones aware of the strain between them.

Lynn called them to dinner, and Ashley preceded the men into the room. She knew Ryder was close behind her, felt the slight pressure of his hand on her back. She cursed the awareness that raced through her every time he touched her.

Ryder seated her in the chair across from his as everyone took their own place at the table. Ashley tensed at having to face him the entire time.

The meal proved less nerve-racking than she had imagined it would be. Lynn talked most of the time, asking Ashley a few questions, enough apparently to satisfy her curiosity, but not too many to seem nosy, Ashley thought. She noticed that both Deke and Jake listened when she spoke and seemed interested in what she had to say.

Ashley glanced at Ryder a couple of times, but as far as she could tell, he never looked in her direction. He almost seemed to be ignoring her presence. When Lynn asked when the baby was due, an uncomfortable silence fell in the room.

Ashley wasn't sure how much Ryder had told his family about how they'd met and how long they'd known each other. She was embarrassed that even Deke knew. A soft blush rose to her cheeks. Though Ashley wasn't ashamed that she was pregnant, there were times she wished it were under different circumstances.

"In about four and a half months," Ashley answered, finally finding her voice. Her gaze went automatically to Ryder as Jake and Deke took turns teasing him about being a daddy.

Ryder finished chewing his food, then gave his brothers a pointed look. "All right, that's enough." His voice was rougher than he'd intended. He knew he had a sour attitude. He just couldn't get a handle on his emotions.

His feelings for Ashley were all tangled up with his feelings for the baby. And he'd been annoyed ever since he'd walked into the kitchen and seen Ashley laughing with Deke. They were closer in age and it had looked like they were really enjoying each other's company. It bothered the hell out of him, and the fact that he cared irritated him, as well. "I think I'll take a look at Blaze. Excuse me." Abruptly he got up and left the table.

The tension in the room was thick. Ashley put her fork down, unable to eat another bite. "I'm really sorry," she said. Her worried gaze flickered between them. "I think maybe it would be best if I left."

"None of us want you to do that, Ashley," Jake replied. There was an air of authority in his tone. Both Lynn and Deke quickly agreed, reassuring her that she was welcome in their home.

Ashley felt tears sting her eyes. "I appreciate your saying that, but—"

"Don't worry about Ryder," Jake said, his gaze locking with Ashley's. "He's always needed time to work through what's bothering him. We've learned to give him a little space. I suggest you do the same. He'll come around."

"And we're all looking forward to our first niece or nephew," Lynn chimed in, her eagerness quite evident in her cheery grin.

Ashley tried to smile as she wiped the tears from her cheeks. "That's very kind of you to say."

"We mean it, Ashley," Deke assured her. He reached over and squeezed her hand. "We want you to stay."

His words made Ashley want to cry even more, but she held her tears in check. She'd been aching for this kind of acceptance all of her life. It warmed her heart that this family would welcome her, virtually a stranger, so easily.

"Why don't you go upstairs and rest?" Lynn suggested, her voice full of concern and understanding. "I know this whole ordeal must be difficult for you."

Ashley had to admit it had been a stressful day. "Are you sure you don't want help cleaning this up?" she asked, wanting to do her part.

Lynn wouldn't hear of it. "You look worn-out. Why don't you take a long, warm bath. Besides, it's Deke's turn with the dishes."

Deke started to protest, but Lynn cut him off. Ashley thought that for someone so young, Lynn could be a barracuda at times. She took Lynn's suggestion and went to her room to relax and try to think things through.

Once there, she turned on a small bedside lamp, which softly illuminated the room. Restless, she walked to the window and looked out, surprised to find that her room faced the barn and corral.

Deep shadows surrounded the house. The area from the front porch to the barn was lit with large lights and, just outside the barn, she could make out Ryder, who was talking with the foreman.

Unable to take her eyes off him, she watched his movements. At one point he turned his gaze toward the house. Ashley's heart pounded as she moved away from the window. He couldn't have possibly seen her watching him.

Ten

Ten

The next morning when Ashley awoke, the queasiness in her stomach hit her hard. She felt as if a tornado was spinning around inside her. She'd heard some women had morning sickness throughout their entire pregnancy. She groaned, hoping she wouldn't be one of them. She lay still for a few minutes, willing it to pass.

A tap at her door surprised her. "Yes?" she called out. She tried to sit up, but thought better of it when a wave of nausea swayed her.

The door opened, and Ashley's eyes widened when Ryder entered. In one hand he carried a plate with a slice of toast cut in half; in the other, a steaming mug. Ashley smelled the aroma of the tea before he even reached the side of the bed.

He had on the familiar tight jeans and a chambray shirt that stretched across his muscled chest. He looked as though he'd been up for hours. Ashley forced her gaze from his body and looked up at him as he stopped beside the bed.

"I thought you might be feeling bad. I remembered what

you said about needing to eat something first thing in the morning. Since you hadn't come down, I thought I'd bring you some toast." He put the tea on the bedside table, then held the plate out to her.

"Thank you," Ashley answered, her voice hoarse. She took a bite of the toast and chewed.

Ryder shifted his stance. "How are you feeling this morning?" His gaze went over her. Her hair was spread on the pillow, much like it had been the last time he'd made love to her. His body tightened just from the thought.

"Not too good, but this will help," she replied, taking another bite of the toast. Clutching the covers, she sat up slowly and reached for the tea. Ryder picked up the mug and handed it to her. "It was nice of you to think about me this morning. I know you have more important things to do." She took a sip of the tea and sighed with pleasure, her eyes closing for a moment before opening again.

"I thought tea would be better for you than coffee." Ryder wanted to tell her nothing was more important to him than her health and the baby, but the words just wouldn't come. He settled for being sure she was all right. He hadn't stopped thinking about her since he'd seen her at the window last night. The whole ordeal at dinner had caused him a restless night. He knew he must have hurt Ashley when he walked out.

Ashley smiled briefly and let her gaze meet his. "It's wonderful."

"Look," Ryder said, sounding concerned. "Maybe you should see a doctor about this again." She looked as if she was going to protest, and he rushed on, "Isn't there something they can give you to help you get over this nausea?"

"I had some medicine, but I've run out. I think I'll run to the drugstore in Crockett to get my prescription refilled. And I guess I should find a doctor as soon as possible, though I don't think I'll be able to get an appointment with anyone for a few days."

"Why don't you get dressed as soon as you're up to it and I'll drive you into town," Ryder told her. "I'll check with Lynn about a doctor. Maybe she knows someone who can see you on short notice."

Ashley thought Ryder and she sounded quite ridiculous, politely talking as if they were strangers. Ryder seemed to be holding back, keeping himself distanced from her. Well, that was what she wanted, wasn't it?

"I can drive myself into town. I'm not likely to get lost," she assured him, not at all feeling like she even wanted to get out of bed.

"I'll drive you," Ryder repeated. "I'll get out of here now so you can dress when you're up to it. Let me know when you're ready." He turned to leave, walking to the door and opening it.

"Ryder," Ashley called to him.

He looked back at her, his expression blank.

"Thank you. I feel a lot better."

Ryder nodded, then left without saying anything more.

Ashley finished the toast and tea and her stomach settled down considerably. She took a quick shower and dried and braided her hair. She slipped on a soft blue pullover top, then a pair of worn jeans. Only she couldn't get them zipped. It shouldn't have surprised her, but it did. A quick search through her clothes produced a pair of black stretch pants with an elastic waist. Ashley put her hand to her stomach. The baby was moving much more often. A warm glow settled deep inside her heart every time it did.

After putting on sneakers, she went to the kitchen. Lynn was busy cleaning the breakfast dishes. Apparently everyone had eaten and left the house.

"Good morning," Lynn said, and sent Ashley a pleasant smile.

"Hello. I'm sorry I'm too late to help you." Ashley gestured toward the sink, which was just about clear of any evidence that breakfast had taken place.

"No one expects you to get up as early as the rest of us," Lynn said easily. "I hope you slept well."

"I did. Thanks, Lynn."

Ashley's smile wavered, and Lynn said, "I don't mean to pry, but is everything all right between you and Ryder?" she asked.

Ashley wasn't sure how much she should say to Ryder's sister. "We have a lot to work through. Most of the time he seems distant and withdrawn. I'm never sure of what's going on inside him."

"Ryder's never been one to share what he was thinking. When he's trying to work through something, he's usually moody and quiet. It takes some getting used to." Lynn shot Ashley a curious look. "Has he told you about Ariel?" she asked.

"Only a little."

Lynn's eyebrows shot up. "I'm surprised he said anything at all." She looked at Ashley thoughtfully. "You must have caught him in a vulnerable moment."

Ashley frowned. "I can't imagine your brother ever being vulnerable."

"If you had seen him after Ariel left him, you wouldn't say that. I never thought that she was right for him and nearly died when he said he was going to marry her. Though she hurt him, I'll never be sorry that she's not my sister-in-law." Lynn studied Ashley thoughtfully. "She was just the opposite of you. Ariel was spoiled and selfish. She liked having a good time and she didn't care about anyone but herself."

Astonishment covered Ashley's face. "What makes you think I'm not like her. I mean, you don't really know me."

Lynn chuckled. "It doesn't take a genius to see that you really care about that child you're carrying. Why—" and she sounded somewhat awed "—you came here to live without knowing a soul. That's a pretty unselfish act in itself. You're pretty and a bit shy. I can see why Ryder's attracted to you."

"I don't know what Ryder told you about us, but we're not

interested in each other that way," Ashley replied, quick to deny what Lynn was implying.

"Come on, Ashley. I've got eyes. I've seen the way he looks at you and it's not *friendly*. And that baby didn't get there because you don't have feelings for each other," she added bluntly. She walked over and put her arm around Ashley. "Give Ryder some time. He'll come around and he'll love that baby."

Ashley didn't know what to say. To protest what Lynn was insinuating would only give more credence to her assessment. "I hope you're right," was all she replied.

"By the way," Lynn said, "I have a friend who's a nurse and she arranged to get you in to see a doctor tomorrow morning."

"Thank you. It's awfully nice of them to fit me into their schedule."

"Fortunately they had a cancellation," Lynn explained. "But I think they would have worked you in, anyway. Your appointment is at eleven-thirty." She dried her hands on a dishcloth, then hung it on a hook on the wall. Then she turned and faced Ashley. "Ryder went out to help Jake with something, but he said to tell you he'd be back in a few minutes to take you into town."

Ashley nodded. "It really isn't necessary for him to drive me. I'm sure he has a lot to do here. I wouldn't want to keep him from something important."

"Oh, I don't think you have a choice," Lynn said with a laugh. "You know, I'm really happy you're going to take over the accounts," she admitted, her eyes lighting with joy.

"I was worried that you'd feel put out of a job. Ryder said you wouldn't mind, that you'd actually be happy, but I have to admit I still feel uncomfortable about this."

Lynn grinned. "Are you kidding? I'm thrilled! I've been trying to talk my pigheaded brother into letting me help with the horses for months."

"That would be Jake, right?" Ashley quipped. The two of them broke out in laughter.

When the back door opened, they were both startled into silence, a grin on their faces.

"Are you about ready?" Ryder asked, his gaze settling on Ashley. He was pleased that Lynn and Ashley seemed to be getting along. Lynn had never really gotten along with Ariel that well. Ryder had a feeling that she just tolerated Ariel because of him.

Ashley nodded. "Of course. Let me grab my purse." She went quickly to her room, then returned ready to leave. Ryder ushered her out to his truck and seated her. He circled the front, then climbed behind the wheel.

Though he'd offered to take Ashley into Crockett, he dreaded it, too. It was a small town and everyone they ran into would be curious about her. Tongues would start wagging the minute they stepped inside the general store, which had a prescription counter in the back.

Ryder parked his truck in front of the store, and they both got out. As luck would have it, Mrs. Weaver, the town's worst gossip, was coming out of the store.

"Well, hello, Ryder," she said, but her attention shifted quickly to Ashley.

"Mrs. Weaver," Ryder replied, then touched the brim of his hat. Her curiosity was hard to miss, seeing she was staring at them both with her snoopy eyes. "This is Ashley Bennett. She's staying at the ranch," he said.

Mrs. Weaver nodded, her gaze narrowing shrewdly. "Oh? A friend of Lynn's?" she pressed.

Ryder didn't like her pumping him. Everyone within miles of the small town knew each other, so anyone new usually stuck out like a sore thumb. "You could say that," he answered evasively. "Excuse us, Mrs. Weaver. Ashley has some shopping to do." He didn't wait for her response as he ushered Ashley into the store.

Ashley asked about a refill on her medicine, and they had

to wait for the druggist to call the pharmacy in Rocksprings to get the prescription transferred. When it was ready, Ryder walked with her to the register to pay for a few additional items she'd picked up. Behind the counter was a woman close to Ryder's age with red hair that looked like it came from a bottle. She gave Ashley a curious look, then turned her full attention on Ryder.

"Well, hi, there, Ryder, honey. Where've you been keeping yourself? I swear you never come in to see me anymore." She leaned across the counter, and the amount of cleavage she exposed made Ashley blush.

"Roxi." Ryder acknowledged her with an easy grin, then introduced Ashley. "This is Ashley Bennett."

The woman gave Ashley a brief glance. She rang up the items, then took Ashley's money and gave her back her change. She chatted easily with Ryder throughout the entire procedure. As she passed the bagged items to Ashley, she snared Ryder's arm.

"We haven't gotten together in a long time," she said, her voice sultry and suggestive.

Ashley's gaze locked on the two of them. It was apparent to her that Ryder and this woman had a past. Her heart suddenly felt heavy. She had no reason to feel possessive of Ryder McCall. But she did. And she knew her feelings weren't just due to the fact that he was the father of her baby. As much as she had fought it, she was losing her heart to him.

She was so caught up in her thoughts that she hadn't heard Ryder's response as he ushered her out the door. Ashley was quiet and thoughtful as they stopped for gas and picked up stamps at the post office, where she filled out a change of address form.

As they met up with folks along the way, Ryder introduced Ashley and pretty much avoided explaining her stay at the ranch. Though she appreciated him being discreet, it didn't really matter much. In a few weeks everyone would know she was having his baby. Ashley had the feeling they were going

to be the focus of discussion for quite a while, which made
her feel uncomfortable.

Ryder remained quiet and thoughtful on the drive back to
the ranch, and Ashley sensed it had something to do with her.
The people Ryder had introduced her to seemed nice enough,
but she hadn't missed the curious looks and subtle remarks
made about her presence at the ranch.

Wanting to talk about it with Ryder, she ventured, "I'm
sorry if my living at the ranch is going to present problems
for you and your family. I guess we should have thought about
that when we discussed my moving here."

Ryder gave her an irritated stare, then turned his attention
to the road. "It wouldn't be a problem if you'd marry me. At
least they'd have less to talk about. Since you're already living
with us, I don't see what difference it makes."

"It makes a big difference." She looked at him and saw
his jaw clench. The muscles in his neck and shoulders tensed
as his fingers tightened around the steering wheel. "You
thought that I'd change my mind about marrying you if you
got me to come out here," she accused, reading his body lan-
guage.

"You *know* it's the right thing to do," Ryder grated, not
denying it. "This isn't San Antonio. In another month, you're
going to be pretty conspicuous and so is our baby when it's
born. I don't understand why that doesn't bother you."

"It does bother me," Ashley snapped, irritated that he'd
manipulated her. She crossed her arms across her chest and
looked away, avoiding his heated gaze. "But I can't do anything about it. I'm not going to marry you," she said, her tone
unyielding. So she couldn't trust him, she thought. He'd had
his own agenda all along when he'd talked her into coming
to the ranch to live. Just like her father, he'd tried to control
her.

Ryder slammed his fist against the steering wheel. It aggra-
vated him that she wouldn't even consider the idea. "Then I
guess we'll live through the tongue-wagging. I lived through

it once when Ariel walked out on me, and I'll survive this.''
He turned his gaze on her, his eyes cold and distant. ''But
you're the one who's going to have to explain to our kid one
day why he's a bastard.''

Pulling to a stop at the house, Ryder got out of the truck,
leaving Ashley by herself as he headed for the barn. His words
stung, and he wasn't being fair. She cared about this baby and
she was doing everything she could for it. But she wasn't
going to marry a man who didn't love her.

That afternoon Ashley started learning how to do the accounts for the ranch. Lynn spent a lot of time with her and
they worked together well. Ashley really liked Ryder's sister.

Late in the afternoon they quit working to prepare dinner.
Lunch had been an ''everyone does their own thing'' affair,
but dinners were planned and they ate together as a family.
Though the atmosphere between Ryder and Ashley was de-
cidedly frosty, Ashley got along well with Deke, who was a
tease and a flirt. He loved getting a rise out of her, and she
enjoyed their bantering.

As Ryder had warned her, Jake was quiet and harder to get
to know, but he made it a point to ask how she was feeling
and told her often to take it easy.

Despite the fact that she'd gone to bed without talking alone
with Ryder, it was he who knocked on her door again the next
morning with something for her to eat. He left her to shower
and dress and told her he'd be ready to go into San Luis
whenever she was.

They arrived at the doctor's office with enough time for
Ashley to fill out the paperwork with her personal information
before her appointment. When she hesitated on the address,
Ryder repeated his for her. Ashley wrote it down, her fingers
moving nervously as Ryder watched her.

A short while later, the nurse called her name, and Ashley
followed her to an examining room.

Feeling anxious, Ryder watched Ashley disappear behind

the door. He'd dreaded the thought that she might ask him to go in with her, but now he was disappointed that she hadn't. He felt a connection between them that had nothing to do with the fact that she was having his baby and everything to do with Ashley. That was another reason he felt a marriage between them would work. But she'd made it clear that she was determined not to need anyone. Including him.

For the next forty-five minutes, Ryder tried unsuccessfully to think about anything but what was happening with Ashley. He was relieved when she finally came back to the waiting room.

"Is everything okay?" he asked, searching her face.

Ashley hesitated at the receptionist window. "I don't know. The doctor wants to see me again in a week," she explained in a quiet tone, sounding a little worried. She dug into her purse, looking for her checkbook.

"I've taken care of the bill," Ryder told her. He ignored her exasperated expression and ushered her from the office.

"You don't have to do that," she chided him. "I have my own money."

"That's my baby, too," Ryder reminded her. "It's only right that I accept some of the financial responsibility." He guided her to the truck. "Did the doctor find something wrong?" he asked, worried that she had to return again so soon.

Ashley shook her head. "I'm not really sure. He examined me, then said not to worry, that everything looked okay."

Ryder touched her cheek and lifted her chin to look into her eyes. "Then why do you seem upset?" he prodded.

"It's probably nothing," she answered, her eyes intent and serious. "He said he wanted to do an ultrasound. They didn't have time to do it today," she explained.

"That's probably routine," Ryder told her, hoping he was being reassuring when he didn't really know what he was talking about. "When do you come back?"

"Next Monday."

"That's no problem." Ryder waited until she was seated in the truck, then shut the door. He went around and climbed behind the wheel. As he pulled onto the street, he asked her if the doctor had given her something new for her nausea.

"Yes," Ashley assured him. "He thinks I've gone through the worst of it, and it should pass soon."

Ryder nodded. They talked more about the visit as Ryder drove back to the ranch. "Maybe you should put off taking over the ranch accounts until you feel a little better," he suggested, thinking about how poorly she felt in the mornings.

Ashley shook her head. "No, I've already gotten a good start and I don't want to stop. Actually, I'm enjoying myself." It was important to her, also, to keep to their original bargain. This was a job, just like any other.

Ashley turned the computer off and stretched. Her back ached, and she pressed her hand against it as she tried to ease the tension from sitting so long. She knew enough about computers to make learning how to keep the ranch accounts fairly easy. Lynn had been very organized and had spent time training Ashley until she felt confident about taking over. Once Ashley understood the process, it was a matter of keeping up with everything. When she needed help with something or had a question, someone was usually nearby to ask.

She was surprised at how much time it took to keep the accounts straight. She was working an average of five to six hours a day, most of it on the computer, the remainder on filing and other details that kept the ranch running smoothly.

Ashley had assumed that she wouldn't see much of Ryder during the day, figuring his work around the ranch would keep him busy. Instead, he seemed to go out of his way to check on her often. Sometimes he would linger after lunch and chat for a few minutes, and Ashley found herself looking forward to the time she spent alone with him.

The McCalls were a close-knit family and from the first moment she arrived, they had gone out of their way to make her feel at home. Her upbringing, however, was a direct contrast to the McCalls. Where her life had been filled with dissension and pain, Ryder and his family shared an honest, loving relationship.

Family conversations were full of stories about their lives, and though she enjoyed being included, Ashley was often reminded of the differences in the way they were raised. She envied them and sometimes caught herself dreaming of belonging with them forever. Then she would realize the foolishness of her thoughts.

Ryder didn't mention the baby very often, and when the pregnancy did come up, his attention seemed centered on her and how she was feeling. Ashley thought he must still be wrestling with his own feelings. She wanted him to accept their child, to be a loving father. If he couldn't, then she'd have to leave. Her child was never going to feel unloved.

She shut off the computer and walked to the kitchen just as Lynn was coming in. One would have thought Lynn would resent the fact that she was still expected to provide meals for her brothers, but if so, it was never evident in her attitude.

"Hey, Ashley." Lynn greeted her with a smile. "How did it go today?"

"Fine. I think I've got things under control now. And I found that mistake that was throwing the balances off."

Lynn gave her a look of surprise. "Wow! That's great. I've been trying to figure that out for days." She washed her hands and began pulling preparations for dinner from the refrigerator.

"I'm sure you would have, given the time." Ashley took the makings for a salad and retrieved a large bowl from the cupboard. She enjoyed working along with Lynn in the kitchen. She'd never had a sibling, though she'd always wished for one. She and Lynn had hit it off from the first day Ashley had arrived.

"Well, thanks to you I don't have to. You're very smart. I can't believe how quickly you picked up on things."

Ashley blushed as the pleasure of Lynn's compliment

seeped through her. "Thank you." She rinsed the lettuce and set it on a paper towel to drain. "How's it going now that you're working with the horses?"

Lynn frowned and rolled her eyes. "It's tough, but I'm hanging in. Russ is fighting me every step of the way. He's giving me every dirty job he can think of, trying to discourage me. I'm sure he believes I'll get disgusted and quit."

"Why would he do that?"

Lynn shrugged nonchalantly. "He doesn't like me."

"I can't imagine anyone not liking you," Ashley said honestly.

Dropping her gaze, Lynn shrugged her small shoulders. Ashley prudently let the conversation drop as she started grating carrots. After a moment she looked up and caught Lynn watching her.

"Am I doing something wrong?"

Lynn chuckled. "Of course not. I was just thinking that it looks like you'll soon be out of those clothes," she commented.

"I know." Ashley knew that was true enough. "I need to get some maternity clothes. I don't think I can put it off much longer."

"Why don't you shop for some while you're in town for your doctor's appointment?" Lynn suggested.

Ashley started to mention she didn't want to do that with Ryder along, but was prevented from saying so when she heard him come inside. The familiar sound of his boots thudded as he came into the kitchen from the back porch.

"Oh, Ryder," Lynn said as he walked into the room, "Ashley needs to do some shopping when she's in town for her doctor's appointment."

"No, that's okay. I can do it later," Ashley blurted out. She didn't want to make Ryder any more uncomfortable about the baby than he was.

"Don't be silly," Lynn insisted. She looked at her brother.

"You don't expect her to fit in her clothes much longer, do you?" she asked, glaring a him.

"I haven't given it much thought," he admitted. His gaze went to Ashley. She looked embarrassed, her expression flustered.

"Of course you haven't. If you had, you'd have seen to it before now." Lynn shook her head.

Ryder stared at Ashley. She hadn't pulled her hair back today, and the raven strands fell around her face, framing her big brown eyes. His gaze slid lower to her breasts and his body tightened. They were fuller now and he ached to touch her there. Her waistline was just noticeably thicker, her stomach barely protruding, but it was obvious that she was carrying his child.

The thought reverberated through his mind. *His child.* He felt an ache in his chest that was becoming all too familiar whenever he thought of her carrying his baby. And a possessiveness that he wasn't used to feeling. Was this what it was supposed to feel like when a man learned that he was going to be a father?

"I'll take you to the mall in San Luis before your doctor appointment."

"You don't have to do that," Ashley answered, then turned away from him and went back to what she was doing.

Clearly, she was uncomfortable discussing the baby with him. He didn't want her to feel that way, but how could he expect her to feel differently? He'd been behaving like a jerk, and he'd given her more than one reason not to trust him. He was lucky she was even speaking to him.

"I don't mind. We'll get an early start so you'll have plenty of time to shop."

Ashley nodded, and he was glad she didn't argue the point. He had to admit to himself, though, that the last place he wanted to be was shopping for maternity clothes.

True to his word, Ryder ushered her out of the house early on the morning of her appointment. They parked at the small shopping mall, and he escorted her to the maternity shop in one of the two anchor stores. He didn't seem at all uncomfortable. As a matter of fact, he'd been quite pleasant on the way over. Ashley had enjoyed talking with him about the ranch and their plans to expand it into an even larger operation, though she already thought it was huge. She understood now why it took his whole family to run it.

Ashley searched through a rack of shirts and selected a soft pink top, then moved to inspect some slacks on a circular rack. Ryder took the top from her hands and held it for her, along with a few items she'd already chosen to try on. She smiled at him, then turned back to the rack of clothes. She was startled when she moved a few of the pants over to check for her size. Inside the rack, a little angelic face peered back at her.

"Oh, my," Ashley said, staring down at the little girl who was sitting on the floor in the middle of the rack. "Ryder, look," she whispered, calling his attention to the child. She had auburn curls, pink cheeks and big blue eyes. "Hello," Ashley whispered cautiously, not wanting to scare her. The little one just stared back at her without speaking, her eyes big and wary.

Ashley looked around the area, but didn't see anyone who seemed to be looking for their child. She peered down at the little girl again. "Honey, where's your mommy?" This time the child sniffed and her eyes started to well up with tears. Ashley looked to Ryder for help. "You try," she suggested, looking worried.

Ryder eyes widened. "Me?" he squeaked. He hadn't the slightest idea what to say or do.

Ashley shook her head. "Well, she's not responding to me so you talk to her." She moved aside and nudged him forward. "Go ahead," she encouraged.

Ryder put the clothes in his hands on another rack and looked down at the little girl. Her lip was quivering and she was scrunched up almost into a ball. Great, he thought. She'd probably start screaming any moment now. Sighing, he bent down so he'd be on a level closer to hers.

"Hi, darlin'," he said, keeping his voice low so as not to frighten her. He didn't miss the way her big blue eyes studied him. "My name's Ryder. And this is Ashley." Ashley bent down beside Ryder. The little tyke watched them both in silent regard. "Is your mommy lost?" Ryder asked, giving her a smile.

The cherub's head bobbed up and down. "Well, I'll bet she needs you to find her," he said soothingly. "How about we go look for her?"

"'Kay," she answered in a tiny voice. Two big tears slid down her chubby cheeks.

Ryder looked at Ashley who was also staring at him. He winked at her, then turned his attention back to the little girl. She was a real sweetheart, and he bet her mother was frantically searching the store for her. "Can you tell me your name?" he asked, keeping his tone to a whisper.

Her head bobbed again. "Crissy," she said, and her voice wobbled.

Ryder smiled again, pleased that she was cooperating. "Well, Crissy, darlin', don't worry about your mommy. I'm sure we'll find her." He thought he'd try to distract her by getting her to talk. "Can you tell me how old you are?" She held up three fingers. "Good girl," he said, holding out his hand. She took it and climbed out from the rack.

Ryder scooped her up in his arms as he and Ashley stood. Crissy put her arms around his neck and hung on as if she'd known him forever. Her chubby fingers stroked his skin as she pressed her soft cheek against his rough one. She trembled in his arms and Ryder felt an overwhelming sense of protectiveness for her. He looked at Ashley and his chest tightened as the impact of his feelings hit him—he wanted to be a father to his baby.

"Let's try to find a clerk," he suggested, holding Crissy a

little closer. Ashley nodded, and they walked to a nearby sales station.

The woman behind the counter greeted them, and Ryder explained the situation, being careful to involve Crissy as much as he could.

The clerk smiled. "You can leave her here if you like. We'll make an announcement on the speaker system. I'm sure her mother will come when she hears her name."

Ryder started to set Crissy on the counter, but she whimpered and clung to him. Her breathing changed and she began sniffling again. The last thing Ryder wanted was for her to get any more upset.

"Maybe we should stay with her until her mother comes," Ashley suggested, smiling at the child. "Would you like that, honey?"

Crissy nodded her head. Her little hand caressed Ryder's cheek, then moved down and played with his mustache. Even through her fear, she seemed fascinated by it.

"Sure we will," he assured her. Looking into her big eyes, Ryder saw the trust she'd put in him to keep her safe, and it made him feel good. "What's your mommy's name, darlin'?" he asked her. She was busy looking at his mustache as he talked, and he had to get her attention and ask again.

"Mary," she finally said.

The clerk nodded and picked up the telephone. After a second her voice came over the speakers.

Minutes later a woman came rushing up to them. She was out of breath and tears glazed her worried eyes.

"My baby!" she cried. "I've been looking all over for you." She reached for her daughter, and Crissy immediately fell into her mother's waiting arms. "Thank you so much!" she exclaimed, hugging the little girl fiercely.

"We found her in a clothing rack," Ryder explained. The woman looked both relieved and embarrassed.

"You must think I'm a terrible mother," she said. "I don't know how she got away from me. I'm usually so careful."

"I'm sure you were watching her closely. It only takes a moment," Ashley reassured her. "She's fine now. That's all that matters."

"I'm so grateful to you," Mary said again, a catch in her voice.

Ryder nodded. "Crissy was very brave. She told us your name so we could find you." He looked at the little girl and grinned. She'd started to cry when her mother came for her, but now there was a touch of a smile on her lips. "You take care of your mommy, darlin'," he said, touching her cheek. Crissy put a finger in her mouth and nodded, her eyes big and wide. The woman thanked them again, then rushed off.

Ashley turned back to Ryder. "You were very good with Crissy," she commented.

Ryder shrugged, a little uncomfortable with her observation.

"You were," she said again. "I'm impressed at how she responded to you. She wouldn't even talk to me. You were able to get her name and her mother's name. I can't get over the way she clung to you."

Though he didn't say so, Ryder had surprised himself. He'd enjoyed holding the little girl in his arms. He looked at Ashley's stomach. The thought of holding his own child made his chest ache a little. He was actually beginning to look forward to its birth.

They finished shopping, and Ashley left the mall with five new outfits to wear. She had insisted that she only needed a couple, but Ryder had argued that she would be needing more than that soon. They argued once again over who was going to pay for the clothes. This time Ashley was pleased when Ryder finally agreed to let her pay. Maybe at last she was getting through to him.

After a quick lunch, they drove to the doctor's office. Ashley checked in, but hadn't waited long when the nurse came to the door and announced her name. She followed the woman to one of the examining rooms and was told to lie down. The nurse adjusted Ashley's clothing, then put a sheet over her middle.

Ashley was flat on her back on an examining table when she heard the door open. She looked up expecting the doctor, but drew in a sharp breath when Ryder came in with the nurse.

"I brought your husband back," the nurse said, grinning. "He seemed a little reluctant, but I assured him this was so much fun he wouldn't want to miss it." She winked and pushed Ryder toward Ashley. "You can stand right beside her. Dr. Charles will be with you in a few minutes."

She left the room and Ryder's gaze fell on Ashley, his expression wry. "She was pretty persistent, and I didn't want to go into an explanation out there in the waiting room. I hope you don't mind that I'm here. I can step outside if you're uncomfortable," he told her.

Ashley shook her head, feeling both nervous and excited, and a little bit pleased that Ryder had joined her. She knew that it took some courage on his part to do so. "You might as well stay since you're here, unless you don't want to."

Before he could answer, the doctor came in and greeted them. Ashley introduced Ryder as the baby's father. The doctor explained the test to them both, then flipped a few switches on a machine. He spread some jelly on Ashley's stomach and started moving a scope around.

Images began to appear on a small screen, and Ryder watched, fascinated. He listened as Dr. Charles talked about doing an ultrasound. Ryder tried to make heads or tails of the wiggling lines on the screen while the doctor kept moving the scope.

"What is that?" Ryder asked, and pointed to a dominant impression that the doctor had been studying for a few moments.

"That, son, is your baby," Dr. Charles replied, a little amusement in his voice.

Ryder studied the object, then smiled as the image continued to move. "Can you feel that?" he asked Ashley, looking unbelievably amazed.

Ashley grinned, her eyes widening as she experienced what felt like the baby's foot roll from one side of her stomach to the other. "Yes." She watched Ryder closely. He was studying the screen intently, his expression changing constantly. It was clear that he was suddenly very much aware that there was a baby growing inside her. And he seemed utterly in awe of that fact.

Craning her neck, Ashley tried to get a good look at the screen, but wasn't able to see very well.

Ryder grasped her hand as he stared at the screen, watching the dark and light shadows change and shift. He focused his attention on them, then a strange feeling crawled up his spine. These images looked exactly like the one he'd asked about only a moment ago. Ryder's heart pounded as he formed his next question, his suspicious nature aroused. "Then what is that?" he asked, pointing at the screen again.

Dr. Charles turned his attention toward Ashley and Ryder. "That," he said very definitely, "is your other baby."

Eleven

Ryder squeezed Ashley's hand. He wasn't sure if he was trying to reassure her, or needed to hold on to her to keep himself steady. "Twins?" he murmured, his voice shaky. "She's carrying twins?"

"Twins?" Ashley mimicked, her heart stopping.

"You two sound like a broken record," Dr. Charles joked. "Yes, you're having twins. Congratulations!"

"Twins," Ryder said again, then looked at Ashley. "Damn, you're having twins!" He was just getting used to the idea of one baby. Now they were having two!

"You're serious?" Ashley gasped, gaping at Dr. Charles.

"I had my suspicions during your last visit. I didn't want to say anything until it was conclusive," he explained.

As he spoke, Ashley searched Ryder's expression. Time seemed to stop as he digested the news. Then he surprised her by leaning over and pressing his mouth to hers. Ashley's lips clung to his as his tongue made a swift foray into her mouth.

"Would you like to know the sex of the babies?" Dr.

Charles asked, interrupting the intimate moment as he cleaned the jelly from Ashley's stomach and pulled the sheet up to cover her.

"I don't know," Ryder answered, sounding as dazed as he looked. He kissed Ashley again, then supported her back as he helped her to a sitting position. He looked at her as she straightened her clothing, his mind still reeling from the news that they were having two babies.

"Do we?" he asked Ashley, his arm fastened around her.

Still in shock, Ashley shrugged helplessly. She licked her lips, still tasting him. "I don't know." She searched Ryder's face, but couldn't tell what he was thinking. If he'd had trouble accepting that she was pregnant, she could just imagine what he was thinking now. "Why don't we wait?" she suggested, feeling confused and anxious. "We've had quite a surprise as it is for one day."

"Good idea," Ryder agreed.

Dr. Charles nodded and assured them they could find out anytime they wanted by calling him. As he turned off the machine, he told Ashley he wanted to see her in two weeks. He congratulated them again, then left them alone.

Ryder helped Ashley off the examining table. His hands were steady, but inside he was shaking like an erupting volcano. "How are you feeling?" he asked.

"Like the wind's been knocked out of me," she confessed.

"I know what you mean."

They left the office, neither of them saying much. The ride back to the ranch was quiet. Ryder had been thinking of broaching the subject of marriage with Ashley again, and this seemed like the perfect time. Surely she'd be able to see that their current arrangement would never work. They were talking about two children now. He wanted his children brought into the world with his name. He'd just have to convince Ashley that it was the right thing to do.

Ashley was glad that no one was about when they entered the house. She wasn't quite ready to share their news. It hadn't exactly sunk in, and she felt like she was in a daze, still wondering if it was true. Twins! Was she really having twins?

Ryder walked along beside her as she went to her room, and she sensed he had something to say. She just didn't know if she wanted to hear it. He followed her inside, then closed and locked the door behind him, effectively shutting out any intruders.

"Are you all right?" he asked, watching her closely.

"I feel the same," she told him, wondering why he'd locked the door. "I mean, physically I don't feel any different." Her heart was pounding, though. She was both excited and a little frightened.

Ryder's gaze ran over her. "You hardly even look pregnant. I can't believe you're carrying two babies." *His babies.* Ryder felt an overwhelming bond between him and Ashley. He watched her turn away from him and cross the room, keeping her back to him.

"I know you're probably having trouble accepting this. I don't want—" She gasped when she felt him come up behind her.

"Shh," he said, and cupped her shoulders with his hands. He squeezed them gently, then whispered, "I want to ask you something."

Fear of what he was going to say paralyzed her. Ashley struggled to find her voice. "What?"

Ryder slid his hands down her arms and across her body to her stomach. "Would you let me feel my babies move?"

His warm breath fanned her face as he pressed himself against her. Ashley felt weak at the knees. She closed her eyes and absorbed the emotions rocketing through her, letting him support her weight. She nodded, unable to even verbalize her acquiescence. Giving in to her desire to be held by him, to feel his warmth surround her, she clung to the moment. It had been so long and she craved this closeness with him.

Ryder felt Ashley's body pressed against his and he closed his eyes, a feeling of relief washing over him and easing the tightness coiled within him. He had thought that she might reject him, and she was certainly within her rights to do so. He couldn't blame her. Although he hadn't meant to, he'd behaved badly the last time she'd tried to share the baby with him. His heart swelled. Babies, he amended silently to himself, getting used to the thought of having two of them.

Ryder held her to him and waited without speaking, his hand caressing her stomach. He thought he felt a faint movement, but wasn't sure. Without asking, he slipped his hands inside the elastic waistband of her pants and over her bare skin.

Ashley felt the warmth of Ryder's hands at the base of her stomach. They were so large, they covered it entirely, his fingers almost touching her femininity. Awareness, strong and urgent snaked through her, building in strength as it consumed her body. It felt so good to be in his arms again. Too good, she thought, her heart aching. If only he loved her as she loved him.

She heard Ryder sigh, and his hard body relaxed against her. She gasped when the babies moved, expecting him to jerk away. Tensing, she held her breath and turned her head to the side, trying to gauge his reaction.

"That's incredible," Ryder whispered, feeling as if someone had let a rocket off inside him. His babies were growing inside Ashley. Her body was nourishing them, giving them life. He wanted to tell Ashley how much that meant to him, but the words just wouldn't come.

Years of not sharing his feelings had made it difficult for him to articulate the emotions he longed to express. When she turned her head toward him, Ryder touched his lips to hers, taking only a taste of what he ached for. He needed her, needed to make her his, wanted to share this moment, to bind them together.

He kissed her again, his mouth fusing to hers, and his hands slid lower inside her clothing, caressing her upper thighs, skimming the fine curly hair between them. She moved her body against his, moaning deep in her throat as he slowly slid his hands up and inside her blouse to cup her full breasts. She arched her back and her bottom pushed against his burgeoning desire. Hot blood surged through him, hardening him even more, making the ache so unbearable he thought he'd explode.

Ryder bent and lifted her in his arms. He heard her soft gasp as he laid her on the bed and spread open her knees. He slid beside her as his fingers slipped inside her lacy pink panties and stroked the softness between her legs. He gently touched his mouth to her lips and kissed her deeply. Slowly and very deliberately, he trailed moist kisses over her face and down her throat, stopping only when he reached the opening of her blouse.

Ashley looked up at him, her desire fueled by the passion in his blue eyes. She slowly started unfastening the buttons to her blouse.

"Wait," he whispered, his voice husky. "Let me." He stilled her hands with his, then slid the buttons open one by one, examining the tops of her creamy white breasts as he revealed them. She lifted slightly, and he unfastened her bra, tossed it away, then took both mounds in his hands. His blue gaze skimmed over her, perusing her as if he'd never seen her, never touched her. Her nipples were darker, her breasts fuller. He stroked their hardened peaks with his fingers, and they tightened and grew even harder from his touch.

"It's been so long. I love the way you respond to me," he whispered, then kissed her fiercely, his tongue mating wildly with hers before retreating.

He looked up at Ashley's face and watched her as he began to make love to her—her big brown eyes dilated with desire, her lips swollen from his kisses. He turned his attention to her breasts and took one peak into his mouth and suckled it. He bit it gently, then teased it with his tongue before taking it into his mouth once again.

"I remember everything about you. Your taste, your smell, the way you moan when I touch you." As if possessed, he moved to her other breast, circling the tip of it with his tongue, drawing out her agony until she cupped her hands around his head and held him to her. His mouth and teeth took her nipple then and Ashley moaned low in her throat, a fevered rush pulsating through her, her hips rocking back and forth.

She reached for him, her hands in a rush to unbutton his shirt. She groaned when he shifted out of her reach.

"Take it easy, darlin'," he whispered. "I'm not going anywhere."

Ryder watched Ashley's expression, the thrill of making love to her, observing her coming apart at his touch, making him want her even more. He felt her hands in his hair as he moved his mouth down her body, stopping at her belly to plant kisses where she carried the life of his flesh and blood.

His babies.

Emotions he couldn't even put words to rocketed through him. The need to possess Ashley, to claim her as his own drove him wild with desire.

He tugged at her pants and she lifted her hips for him. Ryder quickly removed her shoes, then her pants and panties followed them to the floor. He spread her legs and kissed her thighs, then touched her with his tongue, tasting her essence, wanting to consume her, to make her his in every way.

Ashley writhed as his hot tongue licked her body, her heels digging into the bed and lifting her to him. She was on fire, all the need and desire for him she'd craved since she'd last been with him devouring her.

"Ryder, please," she cried out, unable to control the wildfire ripping through her body. She didn't want this bliss, this ecstasy to take her without him going down the same frenzied path. She needed him inside her, needed to feel one with him. "Please," she whispered again, sounding desperate.

In answer, Ryder covered her with his body, supporting his weight with his elbows as he took her mouth and slipped his tongue past her teeth. He lifted his mouth, then licked at her lips.

"Your clothes." Ashley was barely able to speak the words. Her hands tore at his shirt. Ryder lifted himself from her and rapidly removed his boots and clothing, then joined her again. Instead of lying on her, he slid beside her, then lifted her on top of him. Her breasts pressed against the hair on his chest, the friction driving him nearly insane. Then she slid a little lower and filled herself with him.

Ryder arched as she took him, lifted herself, then came down and covered him completely. She was so moist, so hot, that he felt her liquid fire. Every muscle in his body tensed, the strain of wanting her stretching his nerves. He lifted his head and took her mouth with his, unable to get enough of her.

"Ashley." She lifted her mouth from his and he grated her name through his teeth, the tightness of her closing around him, unnerving him. She fitted him so completely. He moved his hips, and she matched his pace, their bodies fused together in a mad rush for release from the storm surging through them.

Ryder felt her climax, felt the small pulses of her body squeezing his, adding fuel to a fire already out of control. His fingers squeezed the tender flesh of her buttocks as he arched his body and pushed farther into her, rocking his hips, filling her with himself over and over again until he fell into the black abyss that beckoned him.

Sprawled across Ryder's chest, Ashley tried to catch her breath. Her heart was pounding so hard it hurt to breathe. She wanted to look at him, but was unsure of what she'd see. She'd given herself so completely, with wild, reckless abandon. Would he know that she loved him?

She started to move, then felt him tighten his arms around her, effectively pinning her to him. With one deft movement, he turned over and she was beneath him, her body pliant. Ashley savored this moment with him. It felt so good to be in his arms.

After a moment he lifted himself from her and eased his body half off of hers. Ashley reached up and ran her hand over his shoulders, feeling his muscles bunch and tighten beneath her touch.

His voice hoarse, he asked, "Are you all right?" Ryder put his hand on her stomach and felt her tremble beneath his touch.

"I'm fine," she whispered. "But I don't think I'll be getting out of the bed anytime soon," she confessed.

Ryder grinned wickedly at her. "I'd like to keep you here, but eventually someone is going to come looking for us."

Ashley nodded, still reluctant to move and break the intimacy that cloaked them.

Ryder touched his lips to hers briefly and felt desire stir his loins again. How could he want her again so soon? He should be sated, but he wasn't. He'd never felt like this with any other woman.

Only Ashley.

He thought again of asking her to marry him. She'd rejected his proposals before, but he told himself that things were different between them now. She was different. What they had together was different. And they were going to bring two tiny infants into the world. Surely she would see that they should get married.

He raised his head and looked down at her, his eyes hooded, still glazed with desire. Her dark hair was spread across the pillow, black and shiny against the pure white pillowcase. Her skin was tinged with a pink hue. As her fingertips stroked his hot skin, he quivered from her touch, acutely aware of her power over him. She was absolutely beautiful, and his body tightened and convulsed with renewed passion.

Lowering his mouth, he kissed her feverishly, and she covered his neck with her arms, holding him to her until they were forced apart to breathe.

"Marry me, Ashley." Ryder spoke softly, his heart pounding. The words came from somewhere deep inside him, a place where only Ashley could fill. Though he'd been thinking about asking her again for days, he figured catching her at a vulnerable moment improved his chances of her accepting.

He felt her stiffen at first, then her eyes became shuttered as she withdrew her arms from around him and rested her hands on his shoulders.

"Ryder," she began, her voice a whisper as her passion-filled gaze searched his. She slowly lowered her hands to his chest and her palms flattened against it.

"Don't say no." Ryder heard the denial in her tone and felt as if he was falling into a mine shaft with no way out. He couldn't stand to hear her refuse him, to hear her deny what was right for them both, for their children. An unbearable ache centered in his heart. He didn't know it was possible to hurt this bad.

"Ryder, I can't" she said, and her voice wobbled a little. Tears sprang to her eyes. "I'm sorry." She pushed at him gently and he rolled away from her.

"You mean you won't," he challenged, irritation sweeping through him.

Her heartbeat racing, Ashley looked into his blue eyes. She saw the disappointment in them, knew she'd caused it. She didn't want to hurt him. She couldn't deny to herself that she'd fallen in love with him. Or that she wanted to spend the rest of her life with him and his family. But not because he felt responsible, not if he didn't love her.

"No, that's not what I mean." She searched the room for her clothing. There were pieces of it scattered haphazardly around. Instead of collecting it, she climbed off the bed and reached for an old T-shirt that she'd left lying across a chair earlier. Quickly she slipped it over her head and covered herself. By the time she'd turned around, Ryder had pulled on his jeans.

"We've been all through this," Ashley maintained, nervously crossing her arms in front of her, trying desperately to hold herself together.

"Well, why don't you think about the babies for once instead of yourself?" Ryder snapped, his eyes boring into her.

Ashley paled. "That's not fair."

Ryder sighed heavily, tired of trying to convince her, but willing to give it another shot. "Look, I know you've been hurt in the past and you don't want to get hurt again. Believe me, I know how it feels." The hell he'd gone through because of Ariel had devastated him and he knew what it was like to try and get through that kind of pain. "Maybe what we can't give each other emotionally, we can make up with what we do have going for us. We're good together, we enjoy being with each other and we're going to have a family."

"That isn't enough to base a marriage on," Ashley protested.

Ryder gritted his teeth, his temper starting to simmer. "I'm not talking about marrying until something better comes along. I'm talking about living forever as man and wife. I'd be a good husband and father. You have my word that I'd never so much as look at another woman. And I swear I'd never hurt you or mistreat you." He stared back at her, searching for a sign that he was getting through to her.

Ashley let her gaze skim over his muscled torso, the patch of blond hair on his chest, his flat, hard-muscled stomach. She loved him so much she was tempted to cave in and say yes. It would be so easy to accept what he was offering, she told herself. But she couldn't.

Their lovemaking had been beautiful, perfect in every way possible. He cared for her, she knew, and he desired her. He couldn't make love to her the way he did if he didn't, but he hadn't whispered words of love. And that was what she needed most from him. His love. His heart.

Ryder shrugged into his shirt, his movements jerky. "It's the best thing for all of us," he stated hotly, glaring at her.

"Right," Ashley snapped, only too aware that his proposal stemmed from deep feelings of responsibility and sexual desire.

Ryder put a hand on his hip. They'd had this discussion, but that was before they'd found out she was carrying twins. "You can't really want to bring two children into this world illegitimately," he said tightly. "I want our babies to have my name." He yanked on his boots while watching her.

"They can have your name without us marrying. And they'll have both of us to care for them. As you said, I'm already living here so it's nearly the same thing."

"That's not good enough."

"Look, you have to understand. Having two babies doesn't change anything. I told you once that I'm not going to get married for the wrong reasons. I haven't changed my mind."

Ryder's expression was thunderous. He wanted to shake her until she could see past the pain in her heart, until she realized that they needed to do this for the sake of their children. He fought the desire to take her to bed again, to show her that what was between them could bind them together for the rest of their lives if she'd just give them a chance.

He did neither.

Instead he turned and slowly walked out of the room.

Ryder didn't look back as he closed the bedroom door behind him and headed for the barn where he could saddle Blaze and ride out his frustration. He needed some time to cool off, time to think about what to do next. It was plain to him now that although he'd thought he could manipulate Ashley into marrying him by bringing her to the ranch to live, he'd been dead wrong.

Nothing, it seemed, was going to change her mind. Why hadn't he realized that? She had a stubborn streak that he was learning was hell to deal with. If having one baby wasn't a good enough reason to marry him, why did he think that having two babies would make her see things differently?

He rode away from the ranch and headed for someplace to lick his wounds. The bite of her rejection stayed with him, and the pain was worse than he'd ever experienced with Ariel. He'd always been a strong person, drawing on his inner resilience to deal with the heartache life dealt him. The death of his parents had been hard, but he'd lived through it, learning in his own way to get past the grief.

Ariel's rejection had hurt, but in retrospect, he supposed his pride had suffered more than anything else. He hadn't felt for Ariel a tenth of what he now felt for Ashley. After Ariel's rejection, he'd picked himself up and moved on, determined not to be vulnerable to another woman again. And he hadn't been. He'd enjoyed life, taking one day at a time, never worrying about the future and what it had to offer. Never really caring.

Until Ashley.

He hadn't planned on spending the night with a dark-haired beauty that he wouldn't be able to forget. And he'd never dreamed that he'd left a part of himself with her.

Ryder figured he'd created his own living hell. He wanted her, but not without the benefit of marriage. Dammit, he didn't want to admit it, but he was afraid of losing her. It wasn't just the babies anymore, though they were a big part of it. He wanted Ashley. Period.

Hell.

It still came back to the same old thing. She didn't want him. And whether he liked it or not, she controlled his destiny, as well her own and the destiny of their children.

Hours later Ryder arrived back at the ranch. He turned his horse over to one of the hands, then headed for the house, dreading what lay before him. His family would have to be told about the babies. He should have felt excited about sharing the news, but Ashley's refusal to marry him had driven a wedge between them that he didn't think they'd be able to bridge.

When he entered the house, Jake and Deke were already in the dining room seated at the table. Ashley and Lynn were just about to take their places. Ryder took his hat off and walked into the room. His gaze slid over Ashley, then past his brothers and sister to see if Ashley had told them about the babies. From what he could tell, he didn't think she had.

"It's about time you came in," Lynn scolded when she glanced up and saw Ryder tossing his hat on the buffet.

"Looks like I'm right on time," Ryder commented, giving his sister a brief smile. Unable to keep his eyes off her, he looked at Ashley as he sat across from her. Their gazes locked, and Ryder sucked in a hard breath, the feeling of defeat washing over him like a tidal wave. From her hooded expression, she hadn't changed her mind. Well, he hadn't changed his, either.

Hell.

They were at a dead end, he thought dejectedly. She wasn't going to give in, and he didn't know what to do or say to make her see things his way.

"Well, I've been waiting all afternoon for you to show up. I've been pumping Ashley about her doctor visit, but she wouldn't tell me anything until we were all together at dinner." She glanced fondly at Ashley. "Okay, we're all here, so give."

Ashley was still looking at Ryder. She had expected him to still be irritated with her, but she hadn't expected the cold, blank stare he sent her way.

An icy shiver raced down her spine. There was no light in his eyes, no glimmer of the excitement they'd shared when they'd heard about the twins, no trace of the tenderness he'd shown her when they'd made love. It scared her to see such a tremendous change in him.

She'd seen many sides of Ryder McCall. He'd shown her how sweet he could be when he took care of her that first night they spent together, and he'd been thoughtful and caring since she'd come to the ranch. His desire and passion when he made love to her was incredible. She'd seen his eyes shine with wonder when they'd found out they were having twins. And she'd seen him irritated, frustrated, angry and upset.

But the look in his eyes right now was so devastating, Ashley was taken aback. Had she done this? she wondered desperately. Had she hurt him so badly that he'd totally shut off any special feelings he had for her?

"Well?" Lynn prompted again when Ashley didn't answer.

Ashley pulled her gaze from Ryder's and looked at Lynn, knowing she had no choice but to tell them. With her voice barely steady she said, "I don't know how to say this, except to come right out and tell you." She already had Lynn's attention. When she spoke, Deke and Jake stopped filling their plates and looked at her.

Ashley paused another moment, then forged ahead, "The doctor told us today that we're having twins." Her smile was shaky, her thoughts in turmoil. She wasn't sure how they would accept the news and held her breath anxiously.

"Twins!" Lynn screamed, her face bursting with joy. She jumped out of her chair and quickly gave Ashley a hug.

Ashley hugged Lynn back. Apparently at least Lynn was excited about the announcement. As Lynn kissed Ryder's cheek, Ashley glanced at Ryder's brothers, who looked totally dumbfounded.

"I know it's a shock," she said to them in a rush. She sent a pleading look in Ryder's direction, but he remained silent. "We were quite surprised by the news ourselves."

Deke was the first to recover. "Damn, Ryder, you always did have big ideas." He winked at Ashley, then reached over and slapped his brother on the back. "Congratulations, brother."

"Yeah, Ryder," Jake joined in the excitement. "We didn't know you had it in you." He sent Ashley one of his rare smiles.

Ashley relaxed a little, and a grin spread on her lips. "I'm so relieved that you're happy about the babies. I wasn't sure what to expect," she admitted.

"Well, of course we're happy," Lynn stated, still beaming as she slipped back into her seat. "Oh my gosh—two babies! We'll need two of everything!"

As they finished the meal, the conversation naturally turned toward how Ashley was feeling and making preparations for the babies. Everyone talked at once, putting in their own opinions on how to handle the imminent addition of two small infants to the household. Ashley should have felt comforted by their enthusiasm, and she would have if she hadn't been so aware of the change that had come over Ryder.

He accepted his family's interest and comments, giving an answer when a question was sent his way, nodding his approval of certain ideas and generally participating in the conversation. But Ashley watched him as he talked. The smile was missing from his eyes, the excitement understated in his voice. If his family noticed the change in his demeanor, no one brought attention to it.

As soon as dinner was over Ryder excused himself and went outside. Deep in thought, he was standing on the front porch when he heard the screened door open and close. Thinking it was Ashley, he didn't look back. He was surprised when Jake walked over and stood beside him.

For a moment neither of them spoke. Then Jake sat on the edge of the porch railing and faced his brother.

"Want to talk about it?" he asked, well aware that Ryder rarely shared much of what he was going through. He'd practically raised him and knew him better than anyone. Ryder had been the quiet one when their parents had died, never having leaned on anyone, never sharing his grief. Though he usually went off by himself to think things through, Jake thought that this might be one time when he needed someone to listen.

"Nothing to talk about," Ryder said, a noticeable lack of emotion in his voice. He'd backed himself into a corner and there was nowhere to go. It was a fate he needed to accept.

"Something's eating at you, I know. Is it the babies?" Jake inquired. "I know at one time you weren't planning on having any children. Getting the news that two babies are on the way must be a bit unsettling."

Ryder shifted his stance, propping his weight against the porch post. "It's not the babies," he said quietly. "I'll admit I wasn't exactly anxious to have kids, but now—" he shrugged his big shoulders "—I'm looking forward to Ashley having them." He had to stop speaking. It hurt just saying Ashley's name out loud. Inside he felt as if an explosion had gone off and left him incomplete. A part of him was missing. That part of him was Ashley and what they had shared together.

He nodded toward the barn and the expanse of land that stretched far beyond it. There was a forest of trees that edged the enormous pasture, blocking the eye from seeing the miles of territory that the McCalls owned.

"Look out there, Jake. That's our heritage. Land that's belonged to a McCall for more years than we can count. I want my children to grow up here, to love the land like I do. One day I want to pass my share of it on to them.''

Jake nodded. "That's as it should be," he agreed in that sedate tone of his.

"Yeah," Ryder grunted.

Jake gave his brother a sidelong glance. "It's Ashley then."

Ryder sighed, and it sounded as if it came from the depths of his soul. "I don't know what to do," he admitted, finally opening up, needing to bounce his thoughts off someone else, to gain some perspective on what to do and how things had gone to hell. Finally, he turned and faced his older brother. "I've asked her a dozen times to marry me, but she still refuses." He shook his head with disgust and his voice rose a notch. "How can she even think of having those babies *without* marrying me?"

"You being such a prize catch and all?" Jake drawled, his tone wry.

Ryder shot him a hard look. "What's that supposed to mean?"

Shaking his head, Jake chuckled. "You must have pointed out all the advantages of marrying you, huh?" He knew from Ryder's expression that he was right. "Security, a family, a place to live, stuff like that?" he asked.

Ryder shrugged uncomfortably. "Well...yeah."

"What about what Ashley wants?"

"I don't know what she wants anymore," he grated, not liking where the conversation was going.

"Have you asked her?" Jake questioned.

"I just said—"

"Have you asked her what she wants?" he said again, cutting Ryder off. "I know you, Ryder. You're like a dog with a bone when you want something. You go after it like your life depends on it, no matter what the cost, no matter what anyone else thinks. Have you given any thought as to what Ashley's needs are?"

Ryder frowned and his mood darkened.

Jake stood and put his hand on Ryder's shoulder. "I remember when you told us she was coming here to live. You mentioned that she'd had a miserable childhood and how she had no one to turn to. I can only imagine what it was like for her if Jacob Bennett's her father."

"What does that have to do with anything?" Ryder asked, confused.

"Maybe what you're offering isn't what she needs," Jake pointed out. "Think about it." Without saying another word, he turned and went back inside the house.

Twelve

Ashley watched from the window as Ryder and Jake saddled their horses. They were moving cattle today, to graze on higher grass in another pasture. She sighed heavily, assailed by mixed emotions that seemed to have a grip on her, like a winter cold that just wouldn't go away. Though it was September, the weather was still summery. Ashley stared at the trees, the changing colors of the leaves reminding her of the changes that had taken place in her life. It seemed light-years ago that she'd left San Antonio.

She'd made a niche for herself here in Crockett with her newfound family. It was both rewarding and comforting to know that Lynn, Deke and Jake really cared about her and her unborn babies. Lynn took it upon herself to watch over Ashley, making sure she didn't do too much to tire herself. A little mother hen was the way Ashley thought of Ryder's sister. Lynn issued warnings and commands, expecting compliance without any arguments. She was mature beyond her eighteen years. Ashley figured that was due to the loss of her parents and Lynn's having had to learn to accept responsibility at such a young age, regardless of her brothers' protectiveness.

Ashley insisted that she wanted to do her part and was allowed to, to an extent. When she helped with the laundry, Deke suddenly appeared out of nowhere to carry the large basket to and from the laundry room, always teasing her and making her laugh. He would insist on helping her with the dishes after dinner, even when it wasn't his turn—which shocked his brothers and sister. After he'd seen Ashley picking wildflowers, he'd often surprise her with a small bunch, refusing to turn them over unless she gave him a hug, or kiss on his cheek.

Jake had his own way of keeping a brotherly eye on her, which also made Ashley feel special and part of this loving family. He'd frequently ask how she was feeling or if she needed anything. He'd touch her shoulder spontaneously and once or twice, surprising her, he'd put his arm around her shoulders and given her a gentle hug. None of the McCalls could ever know how much their acceptance meant to her. For the first time in her life she felt as if she belonged someplace, that she was loved.

Ashley was kept busy most of the time by working on the accounts and planning and making decisions about the babies. She loved living on the ranch—more than she'd ever dreamed possible. She loved the quietness at night, enjoyed looking up at the dark Texas sky and seeing nothing but stars.

She never missed the city and considered herself lucky to have been accepted into this warm and loving family, so unlike her own. Hardly a day went by that Ashley didn't give thanks for her new home.

Life would have been perfect, had it not been for the change in Ryder. Ashley knew in her soul that she was the one to blame for his remoteness. Whenever they were together, whether alone or with his family, their conversation was strained and tense. She longed for him to hold her and love her, but it seemed that they had lost the special feelings that had once brought them together.

Despite the cold distance between them, Ryder took an active role in decisions that affected the babies. He still took Ashley to the doctor, made trips with her to shop for baby furniture and generally made sure she had everything she needed to be comfortable. He even drove her to see Bess a couple of times.

But the closeness and intimacy they had shared had all but disappeared between them, leaving her feeling that it might never be bridged. Ashley was learning just how stubborn the man could be. She had refused to marry him, and he had withdrawn inside himself, cutting off the emotional ties that had once bound them together.

There were times, though, when Ashley still felt his eyes on her. She would look at him and occasionally catch the spark of awareness in his gaze before he shut himself off. Sometimes he would touch her and she would ache for him to take her into his arms. For a moment it seemed as if he would, then he would turn away from her. At those times, she would berate herself for being so unyielding. Maybe she should have settled for what Ryder had offered.

She did love him so. Perhaps she should have been satisfied with being with him, being able to love him, raising their children together. Maybe he wasn't capable of giving his heart after the way Ariel had hurt him. Ashley, of all people, should have understood his turmoil.

Deke came in the house, the screened door to the front porch slamming and jarring Ashley from her thoughts. She looked away from the window about the same time he entered the room. When his eyes caught hers, his expression told her that he knew why she'd been standing there. Still, the words were left unsaid.

"Hey, little mama," Deke called easily, using the pet name he'd attached to her when she and Ryder had broken the news of the twins. "I've got a great idea. What do you say we take the morning off and fool around?" He gave her a lopsided grin.

Ashley couldn't resist smiling back at him. Deke had flirting down to a science. She thought he must drive the local girls crazy. "Is your arm still bothering you?" she asked. She figured he was at loose ends if he couldn't ride out with Jake, Ryder and the hands. Deke had taken a tumble from his horse a few days ago. True, he'd only sprained his shoulder and arm, but Ashley thought that his pride had also taken a beating. His brothers had teased him unmercifully, getting as much mileage as they could from the incident.

"Naw, not really," he denied, though he winced a little as he slightly raised his arm. "I just think I should play this for what it's worth." He shifted his stance and grinned. "So what about it? Want to take off?"

Ashley eyed him suspiciously. "What did you have in mind?"

"How about a picnic?" he asked. "It's a gorgeous day, not a cloud in the sky, and there's not much of summer weather left. What do you say?"

Ashley was tempted to accept. She looked at the desk. There was a small amount of work undone, but nothing that needed immediate attention. She'd stayed cooped up inside the house a lot lately, mostly to stay away from Ryder as much as possible. A day out in the fresh air seemed too enticing to resist.

"C'mon, beautiful. Let's blow this joint," Deke encouraged.

Ashley blushed, then gave him an easy smile. "Okay," she agreed, moving a bit slowly toward him. "Though why you'd want to take a six-month-pregnant woman anywhere is beyond me."

Deke admonished her statement with a stern look. "We'll have no more of those kind of thoughts. Now, for the privilege of being with me, you get to prepare lunch. I," he said, gesturing grandly toward himself, "will get the car and meet you in a few minutes."

Ashley chuckled. "I knew there was an ulterior motive somewhere," she called at his disappearing back.

Within fifteen minutes Ashley had joined Deke and they were riding away from the ranch toward the north ridge.

They'd taken Ashley's car, deciding that the ride would be more comfortable for her.

Ryder had split from Jake and the hands and was chasing a stray that had gotten away from the herd. As he rode along, his thoughts naturally turned to Ashley. He'd given what Jake had said a lot of thought, though he had to admit he still wasn't sure what his brother had been getting at. Apparently it was something he was supposed to figure out.

Well, hell, the only thing he knew for sure was that not touching Ashley was killing him. He'd really done it this time, he berated himself. By taking such a determined stance, he was denying himself the pleasure of Ashley's body. Not only that, by not touching her, he no longer had the liberty to feel his babies move as they grew in her womb.

Shaking the tormenting thoughts from his mind, Ryder started to turn in another direction when the sun bounced off something shiny in the distance. He shaded his eyes from the glare and spied Ashley's car parked alongside one of the dirt roads that twined through McCall land. Curious, he steered his horse a little closer, then surveyed the stretch of grassy land before him. His jaw hardened as he caught sight of Deke and Ashley. They were sitting together beneath the shade of a large old tree.

Ryder was far enough away so as not to be seen, and though he could hear their voices, he couldn't really distinguish their words. A surge of jealousy hit him as the distant sound of their laughter floated toward him. They talked easily, as Ryder wished he and Ashley could.

It seemed to Ryder that his little brother and Ashley had quite a friendship going. Where had he been when all this had started happening? he wondered uneasily. Had he ignored Ashley that much, that she'd felt the need to turn to Deke? Ryder had to quell an instinctive urge to ride up to them and demand to know what was going on.

He shouldn't have been so surprised, he guessed. He'd seen them before, laughing and joking with each other. But he didn't like it, not one bit. Ashley belonged to him, and Deke ought to know better than to be paying so much attention to her. It didn't look right. Hell, *Deke* wasn't the father of her children, he thought wildly.

Anger clouded his thinking. Ariel had made a fool of him once. He wasn't going to let Ashley do the same. Especially not with Deke. And he'd be damned if he'd stand by and watch his brother move in on *his* territory. Ashley may not want him, but Deke wasn't going to get her, either.

Ryder yanked on the reins, and Blaze whinnied and side-stepped before turning and following his rider's directive, taking him away from the intimate scene. Ryder would deal with Deke and Ashley when they got back. He'd be there waiting for the two of them to see what excuse they came up with as to why they were out together.

Alone.

Ashley was laughing at Deke's foolishness as he pulled her car to a stop in front of the house. She had barely opened the door of the car when she saw Ryder storming toward them, his expression grim. A sick feeling hit her stomach. Something terrible must have happened since they'd been gone, she thought, wondering what. Had someone been injured? Deke came around to help her out of the car, and Ashley took his hand for support.

"It's about time you got back," Ryder growled at Ashley, then cut his anger-glazed eyes to Deke. Furious, he planted himself squarely in front of his younger brother.

"What's happened? Are Lynn and Jake all right?" Ashley asked, sensing something was very wrong. Ryder had hardly spoken to her for weeks. Now he was furious about something, looking so much like a fire-breathing dragon that she thought she smelled smoke.

"They're fine," he grated, then shifted his hot gaze in her direction. "How long has this been going on?" he demanded.

Ashley frowned at him, confused. "What?"

"And you," Ryder ignored her response and rounded on

his brother. "I'm only going to say this once so you'd better listen up good. Stay away from Ashley."

Deke's easy grin slipped a little, then he recovered and protectively stepped closer to Ashley. "Hey, Ryder, back off. We were just out for a bit of fresh air."

"I'll just bet." Ryder pointed a finger at him, fury building inside him like a forest fire raging out of control. "I'm not telling you again—"

"Have you lost your mind?" Ashley interrupted, stunned by Ryder's outburst. She stepped away from Deke, who immediately tried to stop her by grasping her shoulder.

"Wait a minute, Ashley. I'll deal with Ryder," Deke insisted, watching Ryder's fierce expression.

"No." Ashley knew what Deke was trying to do and she appreciated it, but she didn't need his protection. "I can fight my own battles, Deke," she maintained, shrugging away from him.

Ryder glared back at her. His temper had been simmering all afternoon, thoughts of Ashley and Deke alone together running like a bad movie through his mind. "How long has this been going on behind my back?"

"Are you crazy or just plain stupid?" Ashley demanded, staring Ryder straight in the eyes. "Deke just thought it would be nice for me to get out of the house and relax for a while. Is that a sin?"

"Yeah, and it's not as if you've gone out of your way to take her anywhere special," Deke chimed in. That afforded him a sharp glance from Ryder and a warning look from Ashley. Deke held both of his hands up in surrender and backed away from them. Maybe he'd misjudged Ashley himself. From his vantage point, she looked like she had a handle on the situation. Still, he stayed nearby to watch the proceedings.

"I saw the two of you today," Ryder told Ashley, making it sound as if he'd caught them in a clandestine affair. His jaw muscle tightened as he thought about the two of them. "Out there alone together for all the world to see. Hell, he even brings you flowers. I think we've given the town enough to gossip about without you and Deke givin' them more.''

"Have you been following me?'' Ashley demanded, gritting her teeth. She and Deke had done nothing wrong, and she wasn't going to defend their friendship.

"No. But maybe I should've been,'' Ryder snapped.

Breathing heavily, Ashley kept her tone very controlled. "The *only* thing you saw today were two friends spending time together.''

Ryder watched Ashley advance toward him, fury in her eyes. Suddenly the hot haze began to clear his mind as her words sank in. He started moving backward, seeing that she looked as if she could commit murder and he was her target.

"That's not—''

Ashley cut him off, still keeping pace with him as he slowly backed away. "You,'' she continued, her voice as sharp as a broken beer bottle, "had better get your mind out of the gutter, mister.'' She poked him hard in the chest with her index finger.

Ryder stopped moving when he backed into something. "It wouldn't be in the gutter if you didn't go traipsing around with my brother,'' he growled, glaring down at her.

"Traipsing?'' Ashley repeated, her mouth dropping open. For a moment she was too stunned to say anything. She couldn't believe Ryder was accusing her of fooling around with his brother. Heavens, she was six months pregnant! Then her eyes narrowed on Ryder. "You're jealous!'' she exclaimed. He had to be jealous, she thought. And if he was jealous, that meant he did care about her. A delicious feeling ran down her spine.

"Jealous!'' Ryder barked, staring back at her as if she had two heads. "Hell, no, darlin', I'm not jealous,'' he declared hotly, the denial automatically spilling out of his mouth. "I just want you to think about how it looks for the hands and Lord knows who else, to see you running around with Deke.''

Ashley spied the horse trough full of water right behind him. "And *I* think *you* need to cool off!'' Using both of her hands, she gave him a hard shove on his chest, sending him flying backward.

Ryder's arms flailed about as he lost his balance. His hat sailed off his head and landed somewhere behind him. He felt himself falling backward, and with no way to stop his descent, he hit the water with his backside. Water splashed up and smacked him in the face, leaving his mustache dripping. Stunned, he stared dumbfounded at Ashley.

"Now." Ashley took a long, deep breath. "Is there anything else you have to say to me?" A moment of tense silence passed between them.

"As a matter of fact, there is," Ryder yelled, just finding his voice, "I love you, dammit!" The words burst from his mouth. He hadn't meant to say them, but in that moment he knew that he'd been fighting himself for too long.

Ashley's eyes widened. "What...you what?" she asked, not believing she'd heard him right.

"Aw, hell, Ashley, I love you," Ryder said again, his voice a little gruff, as if the admission came hard from him. His agitation still evident, he climbed out of the trough and water puddled the dry ground around him.

"Oh, Ryder," Ashley cried softly, then threw herself at him, her face lighting with joy. He caught her to him and held her tight. "Do you, do you really?" she asked, looking up at him, tears in her eyes. Ashley thought her heart would surely burst.

Still looking a little surprised himself, Ryder tilted her face up to his. "I'm afraid I do." He hadn't wanted to, but sometime when he wasn't looking he'd given her his heart. "Well," he said, when Ashley remained silent.

"Well, what?" She gave him a saucy look.

"Ashley." Her name came out a warning and he glanced briefly at the water trough, then back at her.

"You wouldn't."

Ryder bent abruptly and lifted her in his arms. "Don't bet on it, darlin'."

Ashley squealed as he took a step toward it. "Okay!

Okay!'' She grinned, hugging him around the neck with her arms. "I love you, I love you, I love you."

Ryder let her feet slide to the ground as he kissed her thoroughly. "Now, are you going to marry me or not?" he asked, lifting his lips from hers.

She smiled up at him. "Yes. Oh, yes." His mouth claimed hers again, deeply, hungrily. Ashley sank against him, the pleasure of being in his arms making her feel weak with need. She lost herself in the smell, the taste, the essence of him.

"Oh, I love you so, Ryder McCall," she whispered when he lifted his lips from hers.

"Hot damn!" Deke yelled, throwing his brown cowboy hat in the air. "We're gonna have a wedding!" He walked over and slapped his brother on the back. "If I'd known having a date with Ashley was all it would take to bring you to your senses, I'd have taken her out a long time ago."

Ryder gave his brother a pointed look. "Don't be cute."

Ashley gave Deke a hug, then slipped back into Ryder's arms, thinking all was right in her world.

The feeling of euphoria lasted only minutes. As she stood in the circle of Ryder's embrace, a long black limousine came up the road toward the house, billowing a huge cloud of dust behind it.

"Oh, my," Ashley murmured, a feeling of dread coming over her. Suddenly, within seconds, her stomach was in knots. She had become so comfortable living here, that she'd forgotten all about her life in San Antonio. She didn't doubt that whoever was in that car, was here to see her. Trembling, she pressed closer to Ryder, hoping, praying she was wrong. "Ryder, are you expecting someone?" Her voice shook when she spoke. Maybe, she thought, it *wasn't* doom riding in that car.

Ryder shook his head and looked into her eyes. "Not that I know of." He had a feeling in his gut that the devil in the form of Jacob Bennett was riding in the black limo. He'd figured that it was just a matter of time before her father showed up. Actually Ryder was surprised that Bennett hadn't shown up before now. He hadn't exactly planned on meeting the man soaking wet, either, but it couldn't be helped.

The car pulled to a stop on the other side of Ryder's pickup. Deke moved closer to Ashley and Ryder, standing beside them as if sensing a problem and presenting a united front. Silence reigned between them as they watched the driver get out and open one of the doors.

Ashley sucked in a breath when she saw her father step out of the car. He was a striking figure, tall and silver-haired and every bit as formidable as she remembered. She nearly fainted when Martin got out of the limousine behind her father. Jacob Bennett approached the three of them, stopping on the other side of the truck when Ryder spoke.

"That's far enough." Ryder eyed the two men with scrutiny, then his hard gaze locked with the older one. "State your business," he told him, knowing it was Ashley's father.

"I don't have any quarrel with you unless you make it that way," Jacob Bennett stated, his tone rigid. "I've come for my daughter," he stated frankly. He said it as if just saying the words had the power to make it so.

Ryder looked at Ashley. Though there was a slight touch of uneasiness in her eyes, he was proud of the way she was facing her father. Her shoulders were squared, her back straight. Even her chin jutted out a bit. His gaze slid back to her father. "I don't think your daughter wants to go with you."

Jacob Bennett ignored Ryder's response and he glared directly at Ashley. "I've had enough of your foolishness. I've given you time to see the error of your ways. Now get in this car." It was a demand that he fully expected to be followed. When she didn't move, his expression hardened even more.

"Martin, here, is ready to accept the fact that you had cold feet," he said, gesturing toward the polished man beside him. On cue, Martin spoke up.

"Don't let a little misunderstanding keep us apart." He said the words as if he'd practiced them, without emotion, without meaning. "I've missed you, Ashley. Come on home."

Ashley was sickened by the saccharine smile that came so easily to him. She couldn't believe how easily the lie slid from his lips. Looking at him with disgust, she wondered how in the world, even in the most desperate of times, she could have settled for such a spineless jerk.

"I'm not going anywhere." She stared defiantly back at her father. His expression was thunderous, and his skin turned a deep shade of pink.

"If you don't get in this car, right now, I swear I'll—"

"You'll what?" Ashley demanded, cutting him off. She shrugged away from Ryder and stepped a little closer, her body still blocked by the truck. "Never speak to me again? Forget that I exist? You see, it really doesn't matter, Father, because you never really knew I did. And you know what? I don't care anymore." She turned and looked at Ryder, took encouragement from the expression of love in his eyes. "I have a new life now. Here, on this ranch, with this man. This *is* my home." Her eyes glowed with love.

"Don't be ridiculous." Jacob Bennett didn't even consider what she said believable. "You don't belong here."

Ashley closed her eyes for a moment, facing reality. She knew it was time to accept that a part of her life was over. She opened her eyes and they were filled with pity. Her father would never understand her, would never know what really mattered to her. What was more important, she didn't care anymore. Her heart no longer held a place for him.

"You're wrong, though I'm sure you'll never admit it because the great Jacob Bennett only cares about himself and what he wants." Her voice lowered a notch. "What's the matter, Father? Did I throw a glitch in your plans? Is that why you've come here?"

"Listen here—"

"No, you listen," Ashley went on, her voice even, her stance confident. "Whether you choose to believe it or not, I'm a grown woman and you can no longer control me."

Jacob Bennett's face turned bloodred. "I'm warning you, Ashley. If you don't stop this foolishness and get in the car, you'll be sorry." He hesitated a brief moment, then declared, "I'll disown you. I swear I will." Another tense moment passed. "If you don't believe it, just try me."

"That just shows how little you know me," Ashley replied stiffly, not even surprised that he would try to bribe or threaten her to his will. He thought money could buy anything he wanted. Well, she had news for him.

"I don't care about your money. I never did." She glanced at Ryder and, as if she'd asked him with unspoken words, he came forward and put his arm around her. "I have everything I ever wanted right here." Looking from her father to Martin, she stated firmly, "Now, I think you both should leave."

Her father started to speak, but Ryder took a step toward him. "Ashley asked you to leave, sir. She did it nicely." As he spoke, his tone was deadly. "Now, I'm telling you to go. You're on McCall land and you're not welcome." His glance slid to the younger man. "And take this piece of slime with you."

The older man's eyes warred scarcely a moment with Ryder's menacing gaze before he realized the threat implied by his words. He took a slow step backward, then headed for the car, calling under his breath for Martin to follow him. The driver closed the door behind them, then got in and started the car. Ashley, Ryder and Deke watched as the limousine made a large circle and headed away from the house.

Looking at Ashley, Ryder realized how much her father must have hurt her. He put his arm around her. "Ashley, darlin', I'm sorry. He'll never know what he's done," he said, thinking about the man and cursing him for being a fool and giving up a wonderful daughter he would never know.

She put her arms around Ryder and he hugged her closer. His palm caressed her back and her heart swelled with her love for him. She thought about how much her life had changed and happiness spread through her, warming her and filling her completely.

"I love you," she said, looking up at Ryder.

"I love you more," he answered easily and kissed her.

He lifted his mouth and Ashley closed her eyes and rested her cheek against his chest. She'd found a wonderful man who loved her and together they would raise their babies, showering them with love and attention. She'd gained a family whose acceptance and support came as easily as taking a breath.

She had everything she'd ever really wanted.

Epilogue

Ashley stood quietly beside the two matching bassinets where her babies lay sleeping. Though both of them had dark hair like her, they shared their father's baby blue eyes. Just over three months old, Michelle and Melissa had come into the world in their own special way. Michelle had been born first and she'd let everyone know of her presence right away, screaming and wanting her demands met immediately. Melissa had made her entrance serenely and with great poise, perfectly content to let her sister lead the way.

Hearing the thud of boots coming down the hallway, Ashley turned to see Ryder walk into the room. A warm feeling rushed over her as he came to her and she lifted her mouth to his. His kiss was hot and possessive, fueling a desire between them that was as consuming as it was captivating.

Even with a houseful of help, two tiny infants demanded an unbelievable amount of attention. She and Ryder had resorted to taking advantage of every spare moment that came their way. Ashley kissed him back hungrily, giving him her heart and soul. She couldn't imagine her life without him.

"Mmm," she murmured, her lips clinging to his for one more taste of him. Ryder's tongue made a swift foray into her mouth before he raised his head.

"You taste wonderful," he whispered into her mouth, then kissed her again and his heart swelled. They'd been married in a small, intimate ceremony at the house before the babies were born. Ryder had fallen in love with Ashley all over again when he'd looked into her eyes and said his vows.

"Are you sorry?" Ashley asked, her eyes searching his as she looked up at him. He'd told her at least a million times that he loved her, and she loved him so much that it hurt. Still, today especially, she needed to hear it again.

Ryder's eyes locked with hers and he frowned. "What? For loving you?" he questioned. He slid his hand behind her neck, then lifted her chin with his thumb, rubbing it gently over her tender, swollen lips. "Darlin', I could never be sorry for falling in love with you. I'm only sorry it took me so long to figure it out."

When she would have looked away, he gently held her face in place. "What's troubling you?" he asked, his curious gaze sweeping her face, taking in the troubled expression in her eyes. "Have you heard from your father?" he asked, and his voice hardened just a notch.

Ashley shook her head. "No." She pressed herself closer to her husband, seeking his warmth and needing to feel his strength. "I do wonder sometimes if he'll cause trouble for us." They'd discussed the possibility of problems with her father, and Ryder had tried to dismiss her fears.

"You don't need to worry about him, Ashley," Ryder told her. She seemed a little distressed and he wanted to allay her fears for good. "We're married and these are *our* beautiful daughters. Just because your father has money, doesn't mean he could ever really threaten us." He pulled her closer to him. "Our holdings aren't meager by any stretch of the word, and we have connections with some pretty powerful people ourselves. I promise that you'll never have to see him unless you want to.''

"I know."

She shook her head and smiled, yet Ryder suspected something was still troubling her. He turned and looked at his sleeping daughters. "I can't believe how much they've grown in just three months. It seems like only yesterday that they were born."

Ashley giggled, forgetting her troubles for a moment. "The three of you did cause quite a commotion." Thinking about when she'd delivered the babies always made her laugh. Her labor had been long, thirteen hours, and Ryder had been with her every minute. He'd held her hand, bathed her face and fed her ice chips.

It wasn't until Michelle had entered the world that chaos had taken place. The doctor had called Ryder down to see his first daughter being born. Ryder had taken one look at her, smiled, then he'd promptly fainted. Ashley had screamed and Melissa had been born. The nurses had been quite busy, tending to the two newborns and their daddy.

Ryder fixed her with a warning stare. "Don't even start," he advised her. He glowered and a flush crawled up his neck. He'd been the butt of jokes for weeks before his brothers had finally let it go. They still brought it up whenever someone new stopped by to see the babies.

Ashley laughed, then tried to dodge Ryder as he grabbed her and started tickling her. She squealed, slapping at his hands.

"Stop! All right, all right, I'm sorry," she pleaded, panting and trying to catch her breath. Ryder stopped tickling her, then held her to him.

Michelle took that moment to cry, and they both glanced at the wiggling bundle. "I'll get her," Ryder said, letting Ashley go. He leaned down and lifted the baby in his arms. She gurgled, then fixed her eyes on her father, quieting immediately.

"You're going to spoil her," Ashley told him. His expression softened as he gazed at his daughter. Her heart grew bigger as she watched the two of them bond.

"That's my right as her daddy," Ryder quipped.

Ashley leaned up and kissed him. Their lips clung, his tongue seeking and finding hers. His lips were soft and sensual, his taste enticing.

"Careful, my bride," he teased, his baby blue eyes sparkling. "This is what got us into trouble to begin with." He grinned and added, "I told you I'd get the hang of this if you just gave me some time."

"Yes, you did." She still worried about it sometimes. She remembered the day that Ryder had told her he didn't want children. It stuck in her mind like bubble gum to a shoe in the middle of summer. "I know how you felt about having children."

Something in her voice, a hesitancy, made Ryder look at her. He'd learned his wife's habits and knew that when she avoided looking at him, something was troubling her.

"I love these babies, Ashley. Don't ever think that I don't. Before I knew you, I was afraid to love, afraid that someone would love me back and then I'd lose them. I'll admit it took me a while, but you taught me that true love is a good thing, something to hold on to." He leaned over and kissed his wife. "The way I feel right now, I think we ought to have a dozen." He gave the baby in his arms a tender kiss.

Relieved, Ashley smiled and picked up Melissa, who had started to squirm in her bassinet. "I'm glad you feel like that."

"You are?" he asked, then looked at Ashley, his gaze narrowing.

"Yes," she said, quite relieved. A smile spread on her lips. "I'm pregnant."

* * * * *

Take 2 bestselling love stories FREE

Plus get a FREE surprise gift!

Special Limited-Time Offer

Mail to Silhouette Reader Service™

3010 Walden Avenue
P.O. Box 1867
Buffalo, N.Y. 14240-1867

YES! Please send me 2 free Silhouette Desire® novels and my free surprise gift. Then send me 6 brand-new novels every month, which I will receive months before they appear in bookstores. Bill me at the low price of $3.12 each plus 25¢ delivery and applicable sales tax, if any.* That's the complete price, and a saving of over 10% off the cover prices—quite a bargain! I understand that accepting the books and gift places me under no obligation ever to buy any books. I can always return a shipment and cancel at any time. Even if I never buy another book from Silhouette, the 2 free books and the surprise gift are mine to keep forever.

225 SEN CH7U

Name	(PLEASE PRINT)	
Address	Apt. No.	
City	State	Zip

This offer is limited to one order per household and not valid to present Silhouette Desire® subscribers. *Terms and prices are subject to change without notice.
Sales tax applicable in N.Y.

UDES-98   ©1990 Harlequin Enterprises Limited

#1 *New York Times* bestselling author

NORA ROBERTS

**Presents a brand-new book in the
beloved MacGregor series:**

THE WINNING HAND
(SSE#1202)

October 1998 in

Silhouette ® SPECIAL EDITION ®

Innocent Darcy Wallace needs Mac Blade's protection in
the high-stakes world she's entered. But who will protect
Mac from the irresistible allure of this vulnerable beauty?

**Coming in March, the much-anticipated novel,
THE MacGREGOR GROOMS
Also, watch for the MacGregor stories
where it all began!**

**December 1998:
THE MacGREGORS: Serena—Caine**

**February 1999:
THE MacGREGORS: Alan—Grant**

**April 1999:
THE MacGREGORS: Daniel—Ian**

Available at your favorite retail outlet, only from

Silhouette ®
TM

FOLLOW THAT BABY...

the fabulous cross-line series featuring the infamously wealthy Wentworth family...continues with:

THE DADDY AND THE BABY DOCTOR

by **Kristin Morgan**

(Romance, 11/98)

The search for the mysterious Sabrina Jensen pits a seasoned soldier—and single dad—against a tempting baby doctor who knows Sabrina's best-kept secret....

Available at your favorite retail outlet, only from

✦ Silhouette ®

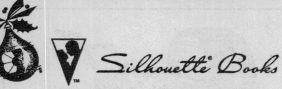

Silhouette® Books

**invites you to celebrate the joys
of the season December 1998 with
the Fortune Family in...**

A FORTUNE'S
CHILDREN
CHRISTMAS

Three Fortune cousins are given exactly one year to
fulfill the family traditions of wealth and power. And in
the process these bachelors receive a Christmas gift more
precious than mere riches from three very special
women.

**Don't miss this original collection of
three brand-new, heartwarming stories
by favorite authors:**

Lisa Jackson
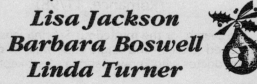

Barbara Boswell

Linda Turner

Look for **A FORTUNE'S CHILDREN CHRISTMAS** this
December at your favorite retail outlet. And watch for more
Fortune's Children titles coming to Silhouette Desire,
beginning in January 1999.

COMING NEXT MONTH